# Lucky the Orphan

Other books by Ray Fisher and Dave Koco

*Operation Freakshow*

# Lucky the Orphan

## A novel

Ray Fisher and David Koco

Hannacroix Creek Books, Inc.
Stamford, Connecticut

Published by:
Hannacroix Creek Books, Inc., 1127 High Ridge Road, #110
Stamford, CT 06905 USA
e-mail: hannacroix@aol.com
Website: https://www.hannacroixcreekbooks.com
Follow us on Twitter: @hannacroixcreek

ISBN: 978-1-938998-38-6

Library of Congress Control Number: 2019940948

Although the ® symbol does not appear throughout this novel, it is hereby noted that these products are trademarked: Nintendo® Cabbage Patch Kids® Dixie® Cups, Snickers® M&M'S® Madonna® WWE® trademark of World Wrestling Entertainment, Inc. Shawn Michaels® National Wrestling Alliance® Backyard Wrestling® Ric Flair® Stanley Cup® Super Bowl® Six Flags® Six Flags Great Adventure® Marine® U.S. Marine® "Once a Marine, always a Marine"® Kool-Aid® "Macho Man" Randy Savage® New Jersey Devils® BMW® Bam Bam Bigelow® Barry Horowitz® Hulk Hogan® Hulkamaniac® King Kong Bundy® Dr. Seuss® Garfield® Spider-Man® Hot Wheels ®*Super Mario*™ *The Legend of Zelda*™ Mike Tyson® *Punch-Out!!*® Pokémon™ *Super Mario Bros.*® *The Mushroom Kingdom* ® *Excitebite*® FORD® Chevy® CORVETTE® 7-Eleven® Garbage Pail Kids™ *The Amazing Spider-Man*® Reese's Pieces® G.I. Joe® Cobra Commander® Baroness® Grateful Dead® Darth Vader®

Please note: There are many meanings for the acronym ACW. In this novel, ACW stands for Atlantic City Wrestling.

*This book is dedicated to those who are capable of viewing the past without rose colored glasses.*

—Ray Fisher

*This book is dedicated to all those who have let me sleep on their floor during hard times when I didn't have a home at different parts of my life.*

—Dave Koco

# A NOTE FROM LUCKY

*Why do people write? For some it's for the money and fame. Idiots. Some write because they just want to be heard. Some do it as a form of escapism.*

*I was injured recently. Bad. I mean really bad. My memories fade in and out depending on the day. My brain and nerves got wacked. Nurse Debbie convinced me to do this. She said it would settle my anger.*

*The injury happened at my job. I am Marine Corp combat infantry. That's not what this story is about though. That is for another day. So, what is this story about? It's about the most important thing in life: family.*

*My sister, Dinker—more on her later in the story—once wrote to me and asked if I was afraid of dying. I wrote back that it's all part of the job. I don't let many people in, so that is why at times this story was hard for me to write because I usually keep walls up.*

*Well. . . I don't know how any of this will pan out, but* that's *the reason I wrote this story. Included in that letter to Dinker, walls broken down, as honest as can be, I told her "I'm not afraid of dying. I'm afraid of being forgotten."*

# CHAPTER 1
## Christmas Day Part 1

The worst thing you can tell a child is that life is fair. Every morning I used to wake up in a godforsaken orphanage named after some goddamn saint. A saint that probably never existed, or at least never existed as he is remembered. Someone whose life story is so riddled with myth it's impossible to tell where the truth ends and the lies begin.

I would always stare at the top bunk and wonder if the world would be better off without me. Now, when I say "world" I'm referring to people, of course. I mean, if anyone really wanted me here, why was I stuck being an orphan? Why was anyone ever stuck being an orphan? What made us all undesirable in the first place? And, why did the title "orphan" make us even less desirable still?

In my lumpy bed, I would sometimes dream that I was someone special, someone desired, some kind of chosen one dispatched by some transcendental authority to Earth. I was a hero sent to save everyone. What was I saving everyone from? It was never any one thing and it was always something different. Once, I rescued everyone from the orphanage as it burned. Another time, it was rescuing people in the rubble of a plane crash, and another time it was taking out a bunch of thugs using only melee weapons. I was always the hero in the dreams. Not a superhero, just a regular boy with great courage, extra strength, negligibly impermeable skin, and resistance to the elements.

Okay, okay, so I wasn't just a *regular* boy. The thing that sucked? I could never finish the dreams. They always ended with some fat nun shaking me awake so I could go to school and be reminded how unimportant I really was.

I remember school. Where everyone had their friends

and they were all so cliquey. I'm not much to look at now, nor was I when I was younger, and my oversized-hand-me-down-clothing-not-having-any-parents thing didn't help me fit in any better, though I did try. Honestly I did, but it's difficult being friendly when you're always so angry inside.

I remember a long time ago, at eight, before I started hating everybody. My teacher stepped out for a smoke or something during snack time. I was behind the mayor's—or maybe it was the governor's—daughter. She could have gone to a way better school, but her mother was a popular teacher for the sixth grade class and her dad needed the votes from the "local yokels," as he was once caught saying. She was so cute and she smelled so good, like fresh flowers, and that was even after she got done running in gym class. I remember all her clothes looked brand new. I think her name was Susie or something along those lines. I honestly don't remember.

The day the teacher stepped out, Susie was pouring herself a drink from her Thermos and spilled it all over the floor. I wanted to make a good impression, you know, since I didn't have any friends at the time. I thought it would be wise to play favor to the popular girl. So I told her I would clean up the spill for her. She thanked me and rushed back to her seat. I thought it was odd she didn't help, but, like I said earlier, I was just trying to make a good first impression.

The teacher came in and overreacted. She slapped me on the back and yelled at me. I was already immune to hits from Sister Satan. I told her to calm her jets or something like that, and explained that I didn't spill the drink, but was helping to clean it up. I might have called her a cunt, or maybe I didn't. I may just be wanting to add that part now.

The teacher was furious. She asked the class who spilled the drink and you know what that bitch Susie said? "The orphan did it!"

I shouted that Susie was a frigging liar. Except that every kid took her side and started pointing at me, also proclaiming that "the orphan" did it.

I hated the rich kids and their parents. They had everything: looks, money, and now, thanks to me, a scapegoat. The teacher was a fat, yellow-toothed, ugly person, inside and out. She yelled at me and told me to clean it up, adding an "orphan" like some people use the word "sir" like a derogatory word, or whatever the hell you call them. No one meant it in a good way.

The students loved every minute of it. That teacher was a horrible person. And, to prove it, twelve years later she would be caught on tape choking a kid and slamming him to the ground. There you go, proof. This kid Bucky always used to say "The proof is in the pudding."

I didn't know what to do at the time though, so I just complained under my breath and cleaned up the mess. Then I saw Susie wink and smirk at me. I lost it.

I screamed, "Oh, I did it? I'm gonna damn do it now!" I picked up a jug of fruit punch from someone's desk and poured it on her and her table of friends. For first impressions, that one was a bad start, and in case you are wondering, I ended up not making any friends in that class. I didn't need them anyway. Them and their damn fancy clothes.

I guess it wouldn't matter anyway though because they stuck me in SPED—or special education class—later that school year. (Now hear ye, hear ye! Let it be known that even people who were in SPED classes can write books!)

I wanna jump ahead, something that I'll probably do a lot from here on out, to December of that same year, and one day in particular in December. It was the one day of the year that even we orphans got gifts. Santa loves everyone, whether they have parents or not, or so I thought at the time. I sprang out of bed with that pent-up energy you can only feel in your life as a child on Christmas. If someone could bottle that energy they would become a billionaire and live forever.

I grabbed my younger brother Peewee's arm and yanked him out of bed. He mumbled something about how it wasn't time to wake up yet, but I just screamed "Santa Claus!"

at him over and over again until he had no choice but to wake up and follow my lead. He was groggy at first but gained energy with every step we took.

Peewee is a great brother, but his one flaw is that he always wants to look good in the eyes of authority. And where we lived, that meant the nuns. Other kids would call him Peewee-rican, the butt-kisser. Peewee-rican because he has dark skin but isn't black, and a butt-kisser because, well, that pretty much explains itself.

He always hated being called Peewee-rican so I tried to only use it when I was really angry with him. He might have been Puerto Rican, but who knows. I think he said something about being from Mediterrania, which I now understand as him mispronouncing Mediterranean. But no one really knows what you are when you're an orphan.

Many people have pride in whatever their heritage is. Well, being an orphan was our heritage. It was the one thing that connected us all. That being said though, some kids would come up with the most bogus stories you've ever heard about who their parents really were. One kid swore that his dad was a world renowned rock vocalist for a top ten band. We all said he was bullshitting at the time, but the funny thing is that now I can actually kinda see that as being true.

That Christmas morning, Peewee and I ran to our sister Dinker's room, which was on the girls' floor of the orphanage.

I know, Peewee and Dinker, strange names, right? Well, some orphans refuse to be called by their given names. The names we got from our abandoners, a.k.a. our biological parents. No sense in keeping the name when they didn't wanna keep you. Abandoners might have won the war, but we still had to hold on to our little battles.

Dinker was brushing her hair as she looked at herself in the mirror, something she did way too often. She had a right to admire herself in the mirror. Dinker was beautiful. Dinker was also very skinny, that unhealthy kind of skinny. The kind where her ribs were poking out and looked like one of those washboards you see in old-time pictures. She also had a few bolts loose, as they say. She was crazy. Crazy as in it wasn't time to wake up yet, but Dinker had been admiring herself in the mirror for a good hour, probably. Orphans can't think too highly of themselves, not with the cold reality of our lives. But then again, I would dream I was a superhero; maybe Dinker needed her vanity.

I burst into Dinker's room with a sleepy Peewee. Now, the boys had to sleep together, but the girls had their own rooms, except they were super small. The bed took up half of the room.

"Hey sis, let's get a move on. Santa came with the goodies," I said.

Peewee let out a really loud "Ho-ho-ho!" His energy level was at one hundred percent.

Dinker replied, "My grandparents are coming today, and I'll have way better presents than what you two will be getting."

Normally, I would make fun of her because of her delusions, but Dinker's parents were killed by a drunk driver, and her grandparents had dropped her off at the orphanage with a promise to return. She had believed in them every day for the past four plus years. No matter how much we teased her about them never coming back, she never lost hope and felt somewhat better than us. Because all the other orphans knew we had no chance of being happy.

The last thing Dinker's grandmother said to her was, "You should take better care of your hair and grow it out." And the last thing her grandfather said to her was, "We will return shortly."

Then they left her here and it had been years. I wonder how long "shortly" was to them? I heard when you get older time flies, but I don't care how old and fast their time was flying, you can't use the word "shortly" if two Olympics have passed by.

I always told Dinker that dogs get treated better than us kids. At least when you ditch a dog you don't lie to them. Sure, it might be scary for the dog, but at least dogs don't have to deal with crazy nuns, and don't have to go to school to get laughed at. I'd rather be a homeless dog than a parentless kid. At least I'd be free.

It was Christmas, so I went easy on Dinker and only said, "Okay sis, see you down there later."

Dinker ignored me and continued to comb her long, beautiful brown hair. She had to look her best for when her grandparents returned for her.

Me and Peewee headed down the stairs towards the presents. We came to a screeching halt when we bumped into Sister Catherine Griggs—who everyone called Sister Satan. Sister Satan was pure evil. You could see the hate in her pruney face. Bucky, a kid who slept in a bunk near mine, would always try to freak us out at night by telling us the story of how he once saw Sister Satan's purple-veined road map legs. It scared the crap outta us.

Sister Satan straightened her robes, all the while mumbling enough curse words to make a Marine blush. After that, she shot me and Peewee her evil eye, hoping to scare us away. Not today, sister, not when Santa left us happiness and the small chance we could get the greatest gift any kid in the '80s could ever want, a Nintendo Entertainment System. I smiled at her, not that I was trying to win her over or anything, I just knew me being happy killed her a little bit inside, and that fact brought me joy. Whoever said "kill them with kindness" was a pure genius. Try it next time you are around someone that hates you. Just smile and be over-the-top kind. The feeling you get can't be described in words, at least by someone like me.

I started by trying to explain myself. "Me and my brother Peewee—." But Sister Satan cut me off.

"He is not your brother!" she scolded. "And that skinny little girl who needs to put more meat on her bones is not your sister. You're orphans and no one loves you."

Sister Satan was always so angry and constantly saying horrible things to everyone. The problem with always saying horrible things to people is that your words lose their potency after a while. It didn't bother me one bit, but Peewee was more sensitive as he loved having a brother and a sister. I always used to tell him that blood doesn't decide family, you do.

I always thought to myself that if I was ever as angry as often as Sister Satan, I would off myself. I always prayed and wished she would kill herself. Not in a mean way, but in a way of relief for her. The same kind of relief a family must feel when they unplug a loved one that is suffering on their deathbed, or how each of our parents probably felt when they dropped us off at the orphanage.

Sister Satan refused to encourage use of our nicknames, but was also too lazy not to remember our real names. She would always call us "brats." Funny enough, Sister Satan even had a nickname for her nickname, S.S.

"What are you brats doing down here?" she asked.

Peewee hid behind me, probably looking at his feet like he always does when he's nervous. I'm sure that he really wanted to run, but at the same time he also wanted to get his gifts before the other children. Peewee had a lot of great qualities, but lacked courage and never wanted to stand up to authority. He was so laid back, I think if he was told to report to prison for a crime he didn't commit he would just shrug his shoulders and do the time anyway.

In a really bad British accent, I said to her, "Well, my fair lady . . ."

Sister Satan just rolled her eyes and ground her teeth.

"We're here to see what Santa got us!" I finished.

Peewee had a huge smile on his face and welled-up hope in his eyes as he nodded his head *yes*. He looked like something from a cartoon. Sister Satan, in all her likeness to the Grinch, just twisted her mouth down into disapproval. It looked like her bitter life was going to sag the skin right off of her face. Peewee lost his smile to her ugliness.

She walked away to the kitchen, grumbling at me and Peewee.

"There will be no gifts until after breakfast and everyone is awake, but since you boys are up you can help me with the—"

We made a point of disappearing before she could finish her sentence. We didn't have much, but we had super speed when it came to avoiding chores. As we ran back to our room we could hear her yelling curse words with the word "brats" tagged on the end. It gave us a good laugh. Sister Satan could have easily got us, but as much as she hated us she was still incredibly lazy.

Peewee and I got back into our beds and talked about Nintendo until the other kids woke up for breakfast. We listed all the games it had, from *10-Yard Fight* to *Zelda*, and how long we would play. All we ever talked about was Nintendo.

We finally went downstairs to have breakfast with the rest of the kids. Mornings were slow-paced, normally everyone looked like zombies, like we had no souls, but today was different and everyone had a spring in their step. Breakfast that day was eggs. At one point in my life I enjoyed scrambled eggs. But, aside from that one point, which was very, very short, every day of my childhood, teens, and later on in life in the Marines, I learned to hate them.

Mice have cheese, squirrels have nuts, monkeys have bananas, alcoholics have beer, fat people have fast food, Hispanics have nachos, Asians have rice, and orphans have eggs!

Do you know what the orphans had on this day in 1947? It was eggs. Yesterday? It was eggs. Today? Eggs. And fifty years from now, EGGS!

Me, Peewee, and now Dinker, all sat at the same table by ourselves. This was not common. The nuns would usually split us up because we had a tendency to act out when we were together. Dinker played with her food for a while before going back to brushing her hair. Peewee and I didn't speak, we just shoveled down those eggs as fast as we could. Dinker had a look of disgust on her face and yelled at us.

"You remember what Sister Satan said about breathing while you eat and to slow down or you will have stomach problems as an adult!"

I was too busy gorging on eggs to bother with her at the moment. Peewee was the same age as Dinker—I was older than them both—and despite his quiet ways he was in fact very competitive. He couldn't let it go and came back with, "We all can't be skeletons like you, Miss Skeleton."

The comment really hurt Dinker. She said something back just for the sake of being mean.

"Hey Peewee-rican. How did it go with your parents?"
Peewee snapped.

"Say it to my face! Say it again! I double-dog dare you! "

"Say what? Oh, you mean PEEWEE-RICAN?!"

Peewee was turning beet red. I could see a little vein in his neck popping out. I tried to calm them down before one of them said something that they would really regret.

"Guys, it's Christmas! Let's just drop it."

But neither of them listened. They were just so fired up with rage and out to see who could leave the most damage.

Peewee screamed, "Your stupid grandparents are never coming to pick you up!"

Dinker dived at Peewee from the side of the table and they started punching each other. I still had a mouthful of eggs. I entered the scuffle only in hope of trying to break it up as quickly as I could, but it was too late. Sister Satan was already closing in on our table.

The kids were all shouting about the fight. Sister Satan ran over and beat us quickly with the ruler she always kept tucked away in some forsaken fold in her clothing. She didn't ask any questions and didn't care. She just knew this table was loud, out of control, and she was going to beat us until we were quiet again.

Pause for a sec, I know what you're thinking. I got beat for something I didn't do. Even worse, I got beaten for trying to break up the fight. Well, welcome to the life of an orphan. It wasn't the first time and it definitely wouldn't be the last.

A few pulled ears—and smacks from the ruler later— order was restored. Peewee's face was still very red. Dinker was combing her frizzled hair from when Peewee pulled on it. I continued eating eggs as if nothing had happened. We were the quietest table in the entire cafeteria now.

Nothing was going to ruin my Christmas, or so I thought.

I guess the beating was pretty brutal that day because Peewee and Dinker were on the brink of tears. I never had a problem with crying, but believe me, the last thing you'd want to do in that orphanage was cry. So, one of the first things you wanted to do was learn how to control those tear ducts. Blinking a lot helps. Bucky used to swear by the method of punching yourself in the face really hard to stop the tears. With tears, you could never really excuse yourself to somewhere private to cry. There was no privacy. You just had to hold it in.

Dinker knew this first hand. Her first few days in the orphanage were very rough.

Everyone welcomed her at first, but all she did was cry about her parents being dead. Me and Peewee felt bad for her and tried to give her the heads-up on crying, but she didn't care and cried anyway and even louder. She thought she had earned the right to cry, but she thought wrong. Crying is a normal thing out in the real world, especially after losing two parents, but here it showed weakness and, for some reason, made everyone unruly and angry. I guess the mob mentality at that time was that if you cried it made your problems bigger than the rest of the other orphans' problems.

Maybe we were just a bunch of huge jerks with anger issues?

It was worse that first night she thought she was safe. Dinker didn't have her room assigned to her yet so she had to sleep in the boys' room. The nuns kept an eye on Dinker, but let's be honest, the night watchmen always fell asleep at some point. Anyway, Dinker was crying in her bed, and I guess that was the last straw. The girls snuck in and held her down, muffled her, and all the orphans beat her while teasing her about how crying is for the weak. Some screamed in her face to shut up, some spit on her, but the worst was that some boys peed on her. I'm pretty sure no girl wants to see a boy's private parts for the first time like that.

Me and Peewee felt bad for her and tried to stop it, we really did, but that just led to the big kids holding us down and giving us really bad pink belly. For those that are lucky enough not to know what a pink belly is, it's when a bunch of kids smack your stomach until it is pink and bleeding, and the pain lasts for days. So yeah, that one day that we tried to stand up for Dinker, our stomachs were red with bloody handprints.

I remember during my time at the orphanage, I once overheard Bucky talking about us all being dead on the inside. Well, I guess that's what happened to Dinker too after a while. I remember some cartoon character saying, "If you can't beat 'em, join 'em."

I guess that's what Dinker did, because by the end of the week, she was beating girls for crying as much as she had gotten it done to her.


Peewee and Dinker slowly ate their eggs while staring at each other with hate in  their eyes. I was poking through my ketchup-drenched scrambled eggs and still trying to catch my breath back from the beating Sister Satan just gave me.
And of course I was dreaming of playing Nintendo.

I must have been daydreaming a little too hard, because the next thing I remembered was Peewee tapping me on the shoulder, telling me to hurry up because the others were already opening their gifts. I looked around in shock at the empty cafeteria. It felt like some time-controlling alien had stolen minutes away from me, or at least that's what I always thought when I went too deep into my daydreams and lost track of time.

Peewee knew everything about me, and me him. He just nodded at me and asked, "Aliens again?"

I whispered back, "I think so."

Then, as quickly as I could, I put away my tray of dishes and ran to the big room with our presents and the Christmas tree.

We entered what we called the "big room," which was just a huge communal room with a television, and tables where you couldn't play the board games we had because all the pieces were missing. It was pure madness: kids shredding open presents, snarling like stray dogs, scratching and punching at each other. It was an indoor children's riot with the newspaper that was used as wrapping paper thrown everywhere. No wonder most of the nuns hated us.

Peewee stuck close by me as we made our way towards the tree and the nuns who were really trying to pass out presents in an orderly manner.

"I don't think Santa got us a Nintendo," Peewee said.

I responded with cool confidence, "Of course he did! I wrote him a letter."

When we finally made our way through to the tree and the big box of presents, we spotted Dinker opening her gift. It was a black Cabbage Patch Kids doll. She looked so happy. Dinker hugged that stupid doll the same way a real mom would probably hug her newborn child. She named it Coco Blacky, or as we called him, Mr. Blacky for short. At the time, none of us knew how racist that truly was.

Sister Satan saw us and whipped two presents at our faces. Mine was soft so it wasn't that bad, but Peewee's present, which ended up being something made from die-cast metal, was hard and heavy enough that it left a purple bruise on his face for a few days.

Peewee had one hand covering the welt on his face and mentioned to me that his present wasn't a Nintendo. He pushed a Fast Eddie stock car into my eyes, like he was trying to prove to me that it wasn't a Nintendo.

I hadn't opened my present yet, but judging by how soft it was underneath the newspaper wrapping, it was probably clothes of some sort. I would take a welt on my face any day if it were for a Nintendo.

I screamed at Sister Satan, "This is not a Nintendo!"

She slapped me across my face. Then, she tried to get me with her "twisted Bible logic."

"How do you know it's not a Nintendo?" she said. "Look at it! It is not a Nintendo."

She grinned, and said in a condescending voice, "You'll never know until you open it."

I loved driving her crazy, but she loved making me angry even more. I ripped the smelly newspaper wrapping off with pure rage to prove her wrong. Once it was open, I was never so sad and angry about being right about something before in my life.

"See! It's just a t-shirt!" On the shirt was written the letters A-L-F. "Who the hell is ALF?" I asked.

"He eats cats!" Peewee exclaimed.

"You're not helping, buddy," I said to Peewee.

"You should be happy you got anything at all," Sister Satan said in an upbeat tone. I wanted to hit her.

It's not like the unfairness of the world had never hit me before. But I never expected it on Christmas of all days! I mumbled to myself, trailing off at the end. "But I wrote him a letter . . ."

Sister Satan, loving every minute of my suffering, gave me that proverbial kick in the teeth using an especially sweet voice. "Santa is a lot like Jesus. He only gives one what one deserves."

"I only deserve an old ALF shirt?" I asked her as I

fought a tightening feeling in my chest.

"You deserve nothing! But I guess Santa felt bad for you, you know, being ugly and all."

I looked down at the second-hand ALF t-shirt with the stretched collar in defeat. I had bragged to everyone about how I'd get a Nintendo. Santa failed me, and I had failed everyone else.

Peewee thanked Sister Satan for his gift then slowly walked away playing with his new Fast Eddie car. She returned Peewee a quick compliment on how good of a boy he was and smiled as I walked away, hanging my head.

Santa and S.S. really ruined my day. Peewee and Dinker tried to cheer me up, so we headed outside of the orphanage to see what the rich kids got. Looking back, I don't see how that plan was supposed to cheer me up at all.

Now, no one left anything unattended at the orphanage out of fear that they'd probably never see it again. Knowing this, we took our presents outside with us. This would later prove to be a bad idea on my part.

The ones we called the "rich kids" were actually not that rich, but compared to us they were the neighborhood elite. It didn't take much in Atlantic City to be considered rich in the '80s. The Korean family across the tracks. They were the richest people we knew and all they owned was a run-down deli/convenience store.

As we headed up the street we saw the rich kids riding their brand new BMX bikes around in circles with looks of pure joy on their faces. No one at the orphanage even owned a bike. Dinker just mumbled under her breath, "Freaking Santa Claus . . ."

Once we were spotted, the rich kids surrounded us and started gloating about their great gifts. All of them had new Nintendo Entertainment Systems (NES) with different games, RC cars, the best pro wrestling action figures, dolls, cash, and of course, their new bikes.

After all of them compared their new gifts with each

other they looked at me, Peewee, and Dinker, and asked us what we got. Me and Dinker were embarrassed. We just clammed up and looked down at our feet. Peewee proudly held out his toy and shouted, "I got a new car!"

The rich kids shared a good laugh about how cheap Peewee's gift was and how they got tons of Hot Wheels as stocking stuffers. Peewee didn't seem to care, because he had a slightly used Fast Eddie Hot Wheels car that he didn't have yesterday, and that made him happy. I wished I could be as humble and happy as Peewee was, but that was not me.

One kid in the back joked and told everyone how all the orphans got their gifts from Super-Mart. For some reason, Super-Mart had the reputation for being where poor families shopped, yet we all shopped there. It's not like any of us bought name-brand. I'm not going to lie. I liked Super-Mart and wish I had the money to buy from there.

That comedian went on asking, "What did the bird say when he flew over Super-Mart?" A few kids giggled, answering, "Cheap-cheap-cheap!"

The joke was cheesy and everyone had heard it a million times already. Me, Peewee, and Dinker only laughed so we wouldn't seem confrontational.

After the laughs died down, one of the girls asked Dinker what she got.

Dinker, with a straight face, whispered as if what she was about to say would get her in trouble.
"A Cabbage Patch doll."

"Oh wow, a Cabbage Patch Kids doll! That's actually a good gift," the girl said back. It's like she was surprised that Santa would give an orphan a good gift. Another question followed. "What's the doll's name?"

Dinker flatly answered, "Coco Blacky."

All the kids laughed except one girl, Black Jen. We had what felt like a billion Jennifers in our neighborhood so all Jens had their title. We had a White Jen, White Jenny, Italian Jen, Korean Jen, and of course, Black Jen. Italian and

Korean Jen were the hottest of the Jens if you must know. Black Jen was angry.

"I'm black, and that offends me!" she said, shaking her finger and pouting her big pink lips. I would later find out this kind of character is known as "sassy black woman."

I laughed at Black Jen saying that, because it was funny. It was probably the wrong thing to do. But, to this day, whenever someone starts a sentence off with, "I'm (insert race, religion, or group), and I'm offended," it makes me laugh my ass off like the Joker from Batman. I find some offended reactions to be priceless.

She screamed, this time to me and Peewee. "That's RACIST!" Dinker snapped back, "You're racist!"

I don't think any one of us knew what the word really meant. Black Jen just called everyone a racist. I think she learned it from her parents or something.

The first time Black Jen called me a racist was when I said I liked vanilla ice cream better than chocolate. She called Bucky racist when he said she was "ashy." She called another kid a racist for not inviting her to a bowling party. The best part was that the kid that didn't invite her was also black. Black Jen was a very angry and confused girl. God, I hope she grew out of that, because when she wasn't out saying everyone was racist, she was actually kinda cool.

Black Jen took a step towards Dinker as if she was going to do something.

Korean Jen took a step, placing herself between them, and whispered to Black Jen, "Dinker is an orphan and all they do is fight. Don't you remember what she did to White Jenny?"

Oh, poor, poor White Jenny. White Jenny wanted to show off at Dinker's expense and once made fun of how poor all orphans are. Dinker didn't take too kindly to that and warned White Jenny to apologize. Well, White Jenny didn't apologize, so Dinker tackled her to the ground and smashed her face into the sidewalk repeatedly. Good thing White Jenny's parents could afford a good dental surgeon. Sure,

Dinker might be poor, but at least her teeth are real.

That's the thing in Jersey. It's okay to be weird and different as long as you can fight off anyone who'll make fun of you. If you can fight, they'll still say that you're weird, but at least they'll leave it at that. If you can't hold your own in a fight, may God have mercy on your childhood, because it is going to be long, horrible, and pathetic.

Black Jen stepped down. Dinker spoke into Coco Blacky's ear, "No one is going to talk bad about my baby." She then closed her eyes and swayed back and forth like she was trying to rock it to sleep or something.

Korean Jen, trying to change the subject, asked me what I had gotten. I felt myself turn red. Korean Jen was very beautiful. At that time in my life I didn't really know why I wanted to impress her so much. With the exception of stealing from her folk's store, I just felt like being a better person when I was around her.

"An ALF shirt," I mumbled, keeping the shirt balled up in my hands. I wanted to squeeze it down into nothing.

Everyone laughed, even Peewee and Dinker. Peewee opened his big mouth again, needing to inform everyone that "ALF eats cats!"

"Yeah, that's the second time you said that!" I griped. Nothing made sense to me anymore and I couldn't shut up about it. "Why? Why in Sister Satan's butthole did Santa get all of you Nintendos, bikes, and great toys? All me, Peewee, and Dinker got is Mr. Blacky, a cheap car, and an ALF shirt." I windmilled my arm and threw the balled-up t-shirt. I was aiming for a sewer drain across the street. The shirt fell and caught on the iron grate.

All the rich kids stopped to think, as if they were out to solve a riddle. Korean Jen spoke up.

"From what I know about Santa, he gives us great presents because we were good. You must have been bad, or not so good, and that is why we got good presents and you didn't."

Everyone thought about it for a few seconds. I remembered all the candy bars, comics, and baseball cards I stole from Korean Jen's family's shop, and when Dinker beat up the new orphans.

I dunno what bad thing Peewee did, but Sister Satan always seemed to be yelling at him for scratching and picking at his jigger. It all came together for me then. I stated my conclusion.

"So we were bad and you all were good. Of course!"

A few seconds of silence proceeded. Our brains were busy running through the logic of such a hypothesis.

In the end, no one argued.

Korean Jen invited everyone to her house for hot cocoa and Nintendo. All the kids crossed the street and ran to her house. Me, Peewee, and Dinker were following last when Korean Jen pulled us to the side. She lowered her voice so we'd avoid the shame of what she was about to tell us. She apologized to us and said we couldn't go inside to play. I asked why, and she said that it was because I steal stuff.

I was hurt, but it was the truth. Dinker didn't care. She was the pretend single mother of Coco Blacky now. She had her own troubles and responsibilities.

Peewee's short attention span pulled him away from the details of why we weren't allowed inside. He was at the sewer drain, picking the ALF shirt up with a stick.

Dinker and I walked back to the orphanage kicking rocks and thinking of how to spend the rest of the day. I mumbled curse words to myself—which was something I never really grew out of. Peewee dangled my dripping Christmas present from the end of his stick like he was a donkey following a carrot.

"Lucy, since you hate this shirt so much, can I have it?"

"It is all yours, pal," I said.

"Thanks! Wow, two gifts in one day. What a great

Christmas."

I wanted to yell at him, but I let it go. Deep down inside I wished I could be as happy as Peewee.

"You know ALF eats cats?" Peewee said once more. "Weird, huh?"

"I know Peewee, I know."

I should have said this before, but Peewee loved to repeat the same jokes over and over. That was his thing. After watching the movie *Beetlejuice*, every time we would go into a K-Mart, he would walk by the mannequins, kick at the display, and yell, "Nice fucking models!" Then he'd finish by grabbing his crotch and making a *honk-honk* noise like in the movie.

I wish I could say he outgrew it, but just this last time we were together at a store, he kicked over a child mannequin and uttered the now infamous line from *Beetlejuice*, grabbing his gonads in the kid's clothes section and everything.

A little boy obsessing over a movie and doing it once or twice is one thing. When you're a grown man doing it for the hundredth time it's cause for alarm.

Seeing it always gives me a chuckle though. You've got to admire his commitment to the joke.

CHAPTER 2
New Year's Eve

It was New Year's Eve and I'd felt like crap since Christmas. I was in a funk and couldn't stop being angry. How could Santa not bring us a Nintendo? I just couldn't stop thinking about it. That no-good son of a gun.

We were at the orphanage's New Year's party that had tons of free food from Korean Jen's family's market. There was also tons of stuff from Shop Rite and Wawa in the big room. The older orphans kept coming by and slapping me on the back of the head, asking me where the hell the Nintendo was. And with every smack I got my lips would move to curse Santa.

Peewee had his Fast Eddie car and was wearing the ALF shirt I gave him. Dinker was combing her hair, again. She had Coco Blacky strapped to her in a seat she'd made out of duct tape. Dinker friggin' loved that doll.

Korean Jen was helping her parents unload the free food. Her dad was a normal-looking, older, bald-headed white man, but her mom was a smoking hot Korean babe. Smoking hot enough that you'd be willing to cash in a few decades of your life to switch bodies with that bald white man just to be with Korean Jen's mom.

Korean Jen was cute and all, but her mom was freaking smoking hot. I never could figure how the hell her dad got a woman like that. I remember Bucky told us once that you can order women from other countries in the mail, and they have to marry you or they'd have to go back to their home countries and get punished. Imagine that.

Shewas ecstatic to see me. Korean Jen always made me feel good, because she was the only person who ever seemed to be happy to see me. After we had the free food, she invited me to one of our ever-so-popular neighborhood street parties. I invited Dinker and Peewee without asking Korean Jen first. When I informed her, she didn't seem to be happy that they were coming along too.

At the street party, the adults got loud, touchy-feely, and drunk. The four of us just sat on the curb sippin' some flat cola from our Dixie Cups and watching the fireworks going off down by the casino near the shore. It was getting late.

Korean Jen broke the silence by asking, "What are your New Year's resolutions?"

Peewee was excited and answered first. "I'm going to learn to ride a bike with no hands!" I had always said that riding a bike without hands takes years of experience and that Peewee would probably kill himself. I must have given him a look then. "Just watch, you'll see," Peewee said to me.

Dinker raked her fingers over Coco Blacky's plastic head and spoke.

"Me and Mr. Blacky are going to get picked up by my grandparents and leave this butthole of a city behind us."

Korean Jen interrupted polity, "That's not how resolutions work."

"I don't care what you think, rich girl! That'what's going to happen! Come on, Peewee."

Dinker grabbed Peewee by the arm and stamped away.

Korean Jen forced out a giggle before turning all of her attention to me. Like I was the only person on the planet.

"So, what about you Lucky?" "My New Yar's thingy?"
"Yeah."

"Ah, I really . . . don't know yet. What's yours?"

Korean Jen looked right into my eyes and said, "I want this to be the year I find my first true love."

I had forgotten Korean Jen was older than me and saw the opposite sex in a different way than I did. I let out a nervous giggle and asked her why.

"I think it is time, ya know?"

"Time for what?"

She closed her eyes and leaned into me.

"Wait. I know! I know what I want." The greatest idea I had ever had crashed into my head. It was foolproof. I would have my Nintendo and now I knew how. I jumped up and dashed away. At the time, I had assumed Korean Jen was upset and that was why she was making a puckering face. I mean, I guess in the end she was pretty upset, but that's not *why* she was making the puckering face. Jeez, I was stupid as all hell.

It wasn't my proudest moment, but I had different priorities at that time in my life. And at that very second, my priority was to get to a phone.

I heard Korean Jen yell something about midnight and a promise I had made her. I didn't look back.

I ran inside her folks' deli/convenience store. I was out of breath. I asked to use the phone because it was an emergency. Korean Jen's mom gave me a funny look and said okay, but that she was going to check my pockets before I left.

I pulled out a damaged flyer from my pocket for a Santa Claus hotline. I entered the number and put the flyer back in my pocket.

The phone rang a few times before being answered by some moaning lady. I made sure that I was the one who said something first.

"I'm going to be a good boy for a whole year!"

The lady on the other end of the line said, "I know what to do with good boys. I'm a bad girl."

I know now that the Santa's hotline was turned into a sex hotline by New Year's Eve, but back then I was a bit confused. "Where the hell is Santa?"

The woman cleared her throat. "Oh, God. No, I'm . . ."

"Where is Santa Claus?"

"I'm . . . an elf. Yeah. I'm one of Santa's elves."

"Why did you sound so weird earlier? What were you doing?"

"Umm, nothing much. What can I do for you?"

There was a long pause. I was so confused. "Can you get me Santa?"

"Santa is busy right now, I think."

"Okay, can you give him a message?"

"Yeah. Yeah, I can do that."

"The fat guy screwed me good, but I got a plan. Tell him I'll be perfect all year long for a Nintendo next Christmas."

Then Korean Jen's mom walked in to listen to the conversation.

The elf said, "I will get him the message. I'm sure he will get you your Nintendo, but also make sure to write him a letter and give the letter to your parents so they can tell Santa too."

This was always awkward for me, especially since I thought an elf would already know something important like that.

"I don't have any parents," I said.

Korean Jen's mom grabbed the phone and demanded to know who it was on the other line. I settled on the possibility that the elf must be new to the job. I dunno, maybe I thought she was a temp or something, because I couldn't see any respectable elf making a rookie mistake like that.

Korean Jen's mom slammed down the phone and berated me about how calling a prostitute on a phone sex line is not an emergency.

"Speak for yourself!" Jen's father called out from the stairs. Without seeing his face, I couldn't tell if he was joking or not. Regardless, some shoppers in the store had a good chuckle.

That slippery elf temp, trying to say the North Pole

Hotline is a phone sex hotline.

"She wasn't a prostitute!" I yelled. I knew that word because me and Peewee hired a prostitute in New York City to carry our bags around for us. I didn't know how to use one properly, because by the end of the night she had just taken our money and bags and disappeared.

"She was an elf," I continued, defending whatwas left of the elf's honor.

Everyone laughed. Korean Jen's dad turned the corner and humped the air saying, "I'd do an elf!" He was humping the air so hard he knocked over some computer parts.

Now, at that time, most people in the neighborhood didn't even know what a computer was, but Korean Jen's dad was already tinkering with them. Later, this hobby would make him millions and Korean Jen's family would leave AC for a better place and a better life.

Kinda wish I'd stayed in touch.

Korean Jen's mom yelled at me to leave, so I ran out. Thankfully, she was so busy scolding Korean Jen's dad that I got to sneak away with two Snickers bars in my pocket.

I went outside to search for Korean Jen. The people were already counting down to the new year.

10 . . . I squinted, trying to spot Korean Jen.

9 . . . I screamed out her name but everyone was so loud. 8 . . . I ran up the street looking for her.

7 . . . I saw Black Jen's mom and asked her if she had seen Korean Jen at all. 6 . . . She was drunk and she hadn't.

5 . . . She was an overweight black woman. 4 . . . She had gigantic boobs.

3 . . . She started to stumble towards me.

2 . . . She stood next to me and called me "sweetums."

1 . . . She held me way too tight and tried to play tonsil hockey with me. "HAPPY NEW YEAR!" she said.

She tasted like a cigar.

Black Jen, Korean Jen, many of the other Jens, and neighbors saw it.

This was my first kiss, and you bet I was regretting it already. Almost everyone laughed about it. Everyone got the first big laugh of the year at the expense of yours truly.

Black Jen didn't see it that way, and ran off never to talk to me again. Black Jen was never mean to me after that, she just didn't want to acknowledge I existed. I understood why. I always felt embarrassed about that, but it had to be a hundred times worse for Black Jen.

After the news made its way to Korean Jen she was so pissed with me. I tried to explain to her that Black Jen's mom made the moves on me, but Korean Jen would hear nothing of it.

"How could you? You promised me I was going to get that kiss at midnight."

I kept apologizing, but I didn't know why. Korean Jen taught me a valuable, yet painful, lesson that night: women will make you apologize a million times without you even knowing why or what you did.

Peewee and Dinker snuck back to the orphanage before curfew. I was locked out until Sister Satan went to sleep. Every time this happened I'd have to climb over the fence and sneak to bed, and if I were caught, I'd invoke the wrath of that wooden ruler S.S. always kept on her.

Problem was, Sister Satan stayed up most of the night reading her Bible, or at least that's what we all thought. The reality was that she was seeking answers from an alternative source that no one could have guessed back then.

So I sat on the curb, looking up at Satan's light, wishing for it to go out so I could sneak in. Korean Jen's parents got too drunk and passed out at the market, so she stayed and kept me company.

Korean Jen snuggled up close to me. I was confused as far as to where we were in our argument, but played it off cool and asked her if she was cold. She said yeah, and I put my arm around her. She asked me what my plans for the year were. I told her about being perfect for Santa so he could get me a Nintendo. She just chuckled, like she knew something I didn't.

She told me she had a Nintendo in her room, her big brother, Biggie, had one in his room, and the family shared one in the living room. I was in total shock. My immature mind couldn't picture anyone richer than a family who owned more than one Nintendo, let alone three.

I asked her for one, but she laughed and said I was so funny. I didn't have the heart to tell her I was being serious.

Could you imagine having three Nintendos? To me, life couldn't get any better than that.

We talked about everything we could think of on that curb as we stared at the yellow light coming from Sister Satan's room. Korean Jen told me she wanted to be the next Madonna. She even sang me a song. It sounded wonderful, but for reasons that boys cannot seem to control—and truer than the dirt in the ground—I ended up teasing her by telling her she needed more work.

Why do boys always do that?

Korean Jen punched me in the arm in a joking manner, but it hurt real bad. I rubbed it and tried to act like it didn't hurt me, but it was killing me inside for real. If being the next Madonna didn't work out, maybe she could be the next Mike Tyson.

Then she asked me what I was going to be when I grew up. The question hit me hard because I'd never told anyone this before. I paused.

"C'mon, you can tell me, Lucky." I laughed and said, "A robot."

"Don't be a jerk! Really, what do you want to be?"

"I'm going to join the Marines and die on the front line."

She laughed harder at that than my robot joke. Then there was a moment of clarity for her, and she noticed I wasn't joking. "Why in the blue hell would you do that?" She sounded shocked.

"Orphans are worthless and can only become one of three things: athletes, criminals, or military. Those are our only options."

"So . . . play basketball or something."

"I love sports but, the truth be told, I suck. I can't even make the team."

"Crime pays good."

"I don't want to be a forty-something thief stealing cars from the casino parking lot!"

"Yeah, that would suck."

She paused to think before she went on.

"Why not join the military and not die, maybe college instead?"

"So I can come back and be one of those homeless ex-marines? No, thanks."

"Well, it's better than being dead!"

"Is it? Is it really? Think about it." She looked at me confused, so I offered her an explanation. "Look, I'm just a dirty street rat and no matter what I do, I will always be white trash. But if I can die doing something brave, no one will talk bad about me and I will forever be remembered as a war hero."

"But we haven't been in a war since Vietnam and that was like fifty years ago."

"I don't think it has been fifty years." Yeah, I was a real nerd back then when it came to history.
"Either way, it has been a long time."

"So?" I said. I was starting to get irritated with arguing about something I was going to do anyway.

"As long as we don't mess up, there probably won't be another American war in our lifetime."

She was quiet for a few minutes. We cuddled on the curb. Korean Jen looked at me with an evil smile and crazy eyes like she had the ultimate idea in her head.

"Well, if you're going to die a hero someday soon, how about you at least keep your promise and kiss me, leather balls."

I wanted to say something back, but she kissed me before I could. Her lips were soft and tasted like Hubba Bubba bubblegum. I wish I could say that my first kiss was with Korean Jen. It was way better than my real first kiss: being manhandled by some drunk fat lady.

Korean Jen pulled back. She smelled like strawberries. The beautiful smile she showed me then would keep me up many lonely nights. Her smile had one tooth that was out of place, which she hated because some kids would call her snaggletooth, but I thought it was cute.

"Why are you smiling?" I asked.

"Because *you're* my boyfriend now."

The word *boyfriend* floored me.

"Whoa! Whoa! Just wait a second. I can't be a . . . you know."

"Why not?"

"I'm a, you know . . . well, I'm ME! And you're a rich girl. You deserve so much better than me, an orphan. It would be a sad story if someone as beautiful and smart as you ended up with a guy like me."

I felt good about saying that at that moment, but it would come back to haunt me for years. Though who am I kidding? It still haunts me to this day! Why in the hell didn't I say the right thing that night? I always wished we could have a Reset button on our life like a Nintendo.

Korean Jen was hard in thought. I imagine she was thinking what it would be like the next forty years married to me. She always planned for the future and looked way too deep into things. After a minute or two, she let out a small smile, nodded once, and then agreed with me.

"I am too good for you, ain't I?"

"That is what I've been saying, way too good."

It was quiet again. We cuddled and I was left to my thoughts, and already starting to regret things. I broke the silence by offering her one of my Snickers. She took it, smiled at me, and then accused me of stealing it.

"Of course I stole it. You see this shirt? It used to be your brother Biggie's. He has so many shirts he doesn't even notice though. I steal, that is kind of my thing. As true as the sky is blue.

"I know, Lucky. It drives my mom insane, but I think it's cute. Like feeding a stray puppy or cat."

I let out a meow and we started laughing. As corny as it was, it sure as hell made her laugh.

We played boxball for a while, which you usually play with four players, but it was so late that we played just the two of us. People in more civilized parts of the country probably know it as four square. This was the dominating outdoor game of my childhood.

Korean Jen eventually won that night. I told her that I let her win, but truth is, she was better than me that night. I was too distracted by her. Was she always as good looking as she was that night?

Again, we sat on the curb. This time, she sat a little farther away from me so we couldn't cuddle. I was already starting to miss the cuddling, so I asked, "No cuddles?"

"Cuddling is for boyfriends and girlfriends."

"Oh," I said, though the sentence finished itself in my head as, "Oh *God, what have I done?*"

"We're just friends," she said, using those annoying hand quotation marks.

"I dunno, maybe we can still be more than friends."

My eyes lit up with excitement as an idea popped into my head. "Cuddle buddies?" She ignored me. "We could be brother and sister, like you and Dinker."

I was nervous with my response. "Oh, no. No, no, no, no . . . Dinker would kill you."

"But she's so tiny."

"She is also so crazy."

Korean Jen looked at me, puzzled.

I went on, "Any girl that has tried to be our sister has got a beer bottle, bat, or metal pole to the back of their head."

"Really?"

"Oh, yeah . . . She once threw her friend off the boardwalk *just for asking* if she could be our sister."

"Ouch . . . Dinker is crazy"

"Dinker is crazy," I said, nodding excessively.

Korean Jen retied a loose shoelace on her left sneaker, then sat up straight.

"I got it. We want to be more than friends, but I'm too good for you to be your girlfriend, and Dinker will kill me if we were brother and sister."

"Don't forget about your mom. She would kill us too."

"Okay, so let's be cousins instead."

I thought it over for a few minutes, like it was some big decision in my life, like buying my first car or house.

"Do cousins get to cuddle?" I asked for the helluvit, already knowing what the answer would probably be.

"Nope," she said, "This isn't the deep south like Delaware."

She made a poor attempt at making banjo noises and laughed to herself. I forced out a smile. That beautiful tooth of hers. I couldn't help but notice how great she was, in every way. She was beautiful, funny, and had a kind heart. Her sense of humor really left a little more to be desired though.

"Ok, *cuz*. We are now cousins," she said, speaking in some weird dialect. "Awesome," I said. "I will break the news to Peewee and Dinker."

"Oh yeah, I get to be their cousins too!"

"But wear a helmet around Dinker, just for now. Just in case."

Sister Satan's light finally went out and the great night came to an end.

I had blown my chance to have my first girlfriend be a beautiful girl that was way out of my league. Instead, years later, I got an ugly fat girl who was bossy—but that's another story for another day.

Korean Jen hugged me and we said our goodbyes. She went her way and I snuck back into the orphanage. I tried to forget how smooth her skin was and how great she smelled: Hubba Bubba and strawberries. It wasn't easy but I had to focus on the task at hand, which was getting that Nintendo.

I didn't get any sleep that night. I spent the rest of it writing the perfect letter to Santa.

CHAPTER 3
Lucky the Champion


Before me and Biggie became verbally contracted cousins through Korean Jen, who was his sister, we barely knew each other. The first time we met was in the basement of his parents' shop where he had his own wrestling federation, which Biggie and his friends called Atlantic City Wrestling, or ACW for short. What we did back then ended up becoming pretty popular in the late '90s and early 2000s, though it became known as Backyard Wrestling. To us it was just wrestling, it was unscripted and all real.

It was scary at Biggie's. His parents' shop's basement—or for that matter, Korean Jen's parents' shop's basement—was filthy, dark, and looked like a place where you would get murdered or someone could "have their way with you."

There was only one small light bulb in the middle with a string to pull on for a switch, and despite there being windows running along the top of the wall, they were covered up by black garbage bags. There wouldn't have been much to see anyway; maybe just the feet of passerby. There were boxes stacked up against the wall as high as the ceiling, but Biggie always made sure to keep the middle of the room clear for ACW.   I don't know how his parents ever approved of us getting together to beat the living crap out of one another in a basement, but then again, maybe they didn't know what really went on down there.

Then, the World Wrestling Federation, now known as the WWE, or World Wrestling Entertainment—wasn't running its *Do not try this at home* disclaimers yet, and due to the fact that none of us at the time knew that pro wrestling was sometimes staged, ACW was more of a fight club than a wrestling federation. In the basement there were four foundation poles holding the entire shop up. We used them for the corners of the ring. We even made our own championship belts from aluminum, cardboard, and bungee straps. We used markers and sparkles—yes, sparkles!—to write on them and made them look like real titles.

Biggie was the world champion. Yes, the world champion! Even though he never fought outside of Atlantic City Wrestling. We were young and dumb. The truly sad thing is, that even to this day, there are wrestling companies not much larger than we were back then who do things just as stupid, if not more stupid.

Biggie wrestled first, he always wrestled first. His opponent was Curt, the local bully—just imagine a big white kid with curly orange hair and freckles. A few had stepped up to Curt before, but they all got KO'd. I once had to deal with Curt outside of the arena: when we went to the pit.

In New Jersey a *pit* means a huge area of dirt. Just dirt. They're great for dirt biking or four-wheeling. Once, we hitchhiked a few hours north to Manahawkin Buccaneer Pit and Curt asked me if I wanted to ride on the back of his four-wheeler. I hopped on and he went in a giant circle. The ride was only about five minutes long. Curt got off and told me to wait. He said that he'd be giving me another ride.

I guess he forgot about me, because he didn't come back for two hours. Where in the hell did he go for two hours? I don't friggin' know. Worst of all, he had left the engine running so he was all out of gas now. When he asked me for gas money I couldn't help but laugh, thinking that he was joking.

He punched me in the gut. I argued that I only rode on the back for five minutes. He said it was more like five hours. We debated until I saw that there would be no compromise.

So, I took the unheroic option, and ran away from him. Later that same day he showed up outside the orphanage demanding that I pay or he would beat me up. Sister Satan chuckled and pulled me out by the ear. I told Curt I had no money, to which he reacted as I predicted, and punched me in the face. I got a solid beating. I mean, I've had some good beatings in my life, even after Curt, but Curt really knew how to pack a wallop.

He beat me until Dennis, the king bully of the orphanage, stepped in and said I'd had enough.

Curt was still angry, but respected Dennis's authority and backed off.

You can beat up the weak, but you still have to show respect to the other bullies.

Since I was busy bleeding and not putting up much of a fight anymore, Curt went through my pockets and took what little money I had as well as an old Snickers candy bar and went on his way.

That day at ACW everyone was rooting for Biggie to kick Curt's ass, because winning would only make him a bigger asshole. And that would make everyone else's life even more miserable.

The ring was small, so the ref was always outside of it. That day the ref was Bucky. He motioned for someone to ring the bell. A kid in a wheelchair, nicknamed Muscle Car, shook a tin can with a marble inside. The fight officially started.

Muscle Car was in a wheelchair because of a gunshot wound. I heard two stories: one involving a drive-by, another being an accident when he and his cousin were playing with his dad's gun. I never had the balls to ask him what really happened. He was a nice enough kid, but still, asking him why he's in a wheelchair always seemed wrong to me. I think the rule is: In a cast, you can ask; in a wheelchair, pretend it's not there. What chair? I don't see a chair.

The biggest question I have for myself now is how in the hell Muscle Car was making it down into that basement. Was someone always helping him and I just never noticed? Basement ACW wasn't exactly wheelchair accessible.

Muscle Car always made everyone laugh so hard with his, "It's me. It's me. Muscle Car! Muscle Car! MUSCLE CAR!"

I admired him for being so positive. I had both legs and I was a super-negative motherfudger. I'm sure if I had to be in a wheelchair I would be a world class grade-A prick—as if I'm not one already.

Anyways, the fight: Curt hit Biggie in the mouth three times and got in one good shot on the nose. Biggie's face was now bloody and Curt was more full of himself at that moment than I had ever seen him. Curt was wearing a cocky smile on his face until Biggie wiped it off with the loudest slap I ever heard. I mean, it was like thunder! It sounded like someone dropped ten pounds of pizza dough off the top of the tallest building in our neighborhood onto the sidewalk. Curt took a knee.

I think the pain was something new for him. I'd never seen him hurt like that before. His expression was a combination of fear and shock. He tried to tap out, saying that he quit. Too bad Ref Bucky and Muscle Car both happened to be victims of Curt's bullying. Bucky never gave the signal to end the match, not that Muscle Car would have rung the bell anyway.

Biggie stood Curt up and lifted him up over his shoulders. Curt's crotch was right in Biggie's face. I know this sounds pretty nasty, but if anyone reading this is a fan of pro wrestling you know that this is what we call a *power bomb*.

Curt was screaming that he already quit. Biggie bounced Curt on his shoulders, wanting to give him the dreaded "last ride." As Biggie was turning to throw his opponent down, Curt hit his head on the wooden ceiling beam and was knocked out. Biggie slammed the dead weight down with all his might. It made a sickening thud. Curt didn't move. The room was quiet for a  few seconds. I like to think that in those few seconds everyone was reflecting on whether or not they cared. But even with Curt looking like he was dead, someone broke the silence with a hoot and everyone cheered as Biggie held up his world title. Somebody helped Bucky to pull Curt out of the ring. Then I saw Bucky kicking Curt in the ribs.

After a few minutes of celebrating Biggie's greatness and the fall of a bully, Muscle Car broke up all the high fives with two simple words. "Who's next?" No one was quick to volunteer, not with a KO'd Curt on the side, who was now twitching and drooling on himself. Someone should have called an ambulance.

A kid named Vinnie, who looked like a giant mutated mouse, volunteered to go next. He was the ACW Intercontinental Champion and went by the moniker Vinnie the Ninja Mouse. Can you believe he chose that nickname? He started mouthing off about how no one had the balls to challenge him. I just stayed quiet, hoping to get out of that place in one piece. Just in case you didn't know, watching people get their butts kicked is a lot more fun than getting your own butt kicked.

Muscle Car joined in and tried sweet-talking others to fight Vinnie. Biggie put his freakishly large hands on my shoulders saying, "I heard Lucky knows how to throw fists re-e-e-al good." Everyone was agreeing with Biggie, though I swear none of them had ever seen me fight before. For a few seconds, I thought I was the man. Then I realized they were just looking for someone to take an ass whooping.

No way I was talking myself out of that one, though I did try. I told them that it was my first time and I needed to watch more fights first.

Vinnie gave out a villainous laugh and said I was scared, which I was. I was ready to drop a deuce in my pants. I could be brave in the orphanage, but outside of that, in the real world, I was a quiet and shy kid. The only thing I had that helped me, or maybe hurt me, was my Marty McFly complex. I wanted to say no so bad, but when Vinnie made that clucking sound with the obnoxious dance to go with it, I had to accept the challenge.

Everyone cheered. They weren't cheering for me. They were cheering for the next fight. I stumbled on the bottom rope as I climbed into the ring. The stumble got a few chuckles. I was so nervous, but when Muscle Car rang that bell, I was focused.

I went in with everything I had. I threw a jab, jab, jab and then a huge right hook. Vinnie's nose spurted blood. In Atlantic City we call that a *gusher*. I was celebrating. I shouldn't have been, but I have a problem with confidence, being that I either have too little or too much, but never just the right amount. You think I would have learned something from that first match.

Muscle Car yelled at me, "Turn around, dumbass! It's not over!"

I turned around and Vinnie shoulder-tackled me into a corner of the ring. My back and head hit it hard. It sucked. He went straight to a bear hug. Bear hugs suck on TV because they are boring to watch; bear hugs suck in real life because they are painful.

I wanted to tap. All I had to do was tap out and the pain would end, but the crowd, that damn crowd, was rooting for me not to tap. But the F'n pain was killing me. How the hell can another human being squeeze like that? How in the hell do you even practice that move?

I'd had enough and I was really about to tap, when in the corner of my eyes I saw Muscle Car on the floor next to a KO'd Curt with no pants on. My first reaction was more concern than alarm. I screamed in pure agony, "Muscle Car fell and lost his pants!"

Vinnie immediately let go and everyone all at once turned to look at crippled Muscle Car.

He was wriggling to force his naked butt onto Curt's unconscious drooling face. Everyone was dead silent. It was even more quiet than when we all thought Curt was dead. Muscle Car was making funny grunts and moans over Curt's face.

Given the silence, I think that was the most peaceful the basement had ever been with us down there. I think we were all just trying to figure out what the hell was going on. Muscle Car didn't seem to be in any pain. Why in the hell were his pants off? And why was he trying to sit on Curt's face?

Biggie was the one to break the silence. "Muscle Car, are you gay or something?"

Muscle Car was so calm, like he was doing an everyday chore. Like it was no big deal. "Of course not."

"Then could you please explain why you don't have pants on and have your freakin' butt in Curt's face?"

Muscle Car gave us a big grin. No one could have guessed the next words to come out of his mouth would be "It's simple, I'm pooping in his mouth."

I think that answer confused us even more. "WHY?" someone shouted.

"He bullied me into buying a guitar."

Damn, not the guitars again, I thought. Curt had done the same exact thing to Peewee! How many guitars had this bully made people buy with their savings?

Again, there was silence. I think some people were trying to figure out what Muscle Car meant when he said that Curt bullied him into buying a guitar, so I'll give the simple explanation. Curt would bully people who he knew wouldn't put up a fight. He'd get them to buy guitars for him. I know it's stupid, but that's what he did. You've gotta remember that Atlantic City has less brain cells per capita than any other city, I swear. Leave it up to Curt to bully a kid in a wheelchair.

I'm sure everyone wanted to look away, but couldn't. There, on the floor, was a wheelless Muscle Car with pale ass and legs, snuggling himself sideways on Curt's face to poop. It was so quiet you could hear Muscle Car pinching it out, and that wasn't even the half of it.

Muscle Car used his bare hands to paint Curt's face up with fresh poop, even smearing some into his eyes and mouth.

Jesus Christ, I know adults who are shocked by that kind of thing. Imagine what it was like for us as kids. Muscle Car even peed on him. The piss and poo were all over the both of them, but Muscle Car didn't seem to mind. He was having a ball getting his revenge. Can you believe that while this was going on, upstairs people were buying their lunches and living their normal lives?

I think I snapped out of the Muscle Car crap-induced hypnosis first, and while everyone else was distracted, I snuck up behind Vinnie and rolled him up from behind. His shoulders were down and the referee counted out a super-fast 1, 2, 3! Ref Bucky raised my hand in victory and Muscle Car was lying on the floor, covered in some poop and pee himself. He screamed, "NEW ACW INTERCONTINENTAL CHAMPION OF THE WO-O-O-O-O-RRRLD!"

Up to that part of my life it was the biggest accomplishment ever.

I looked like Shawn Michaels winning his first-ever World Wrestling Federation world title. I was sitting up and looking at that aluminum title with the glued-on sparkles as if it was the most valuable thing in the world. Muscle Car kept going with his announcing, "Biggest upset ever!" He said this over and over, pretending to hold a microphone in his crap-covered hand. He looked so happy. The moment would have been a lot more special for me if he weren't painted in crap. It would have been better still if the whole room hadn't smelled like crap.

Vinnie was outraged and was whining for a rematch.

"It was a fluke! I want my rematch now! Gimme my damn rematch!" "No!"

"What do you mean no?"

"No, this was my first fight and I'm the ACW Intercontinental Champion. That's not how it's supposed to work."

Vinnie the Ninja Mouse looked like an angry bull. Biggie held him back saying, "Let's just see what the commissioner has to say about all of this."

Muscle Car wiggled his way back onto his chair, pulled up his pants, and acted like the Curt thing never happened. He smelled horrible. There was a trail of poop smeared on the floor. Everyone was giving themselves a safety buffer. Muscle Car raised a single finger for attention.

"According to the NWA—National Wrestling Alliance—rules and standards that ACW follows, and your contracts, Lucky doesn't have to give Vinnie a rematch today, but he does have to fight him again within thirty days or be stripped of the title."

For the record, that might sound like an impressive speech for a kid, but don't forget that on top of it being completely made up, it was coming from a boy who had poop smeared on himself. I mean, looking back we can all have a good laugh, but no one was laughing at the time.

I grabbed my title and ran out, being sure to have the last word. "See you in thirty, sucker!"

I was a true heel before I even knew what the hell that meant.

Vinnie was so angry he kicked Curt, who was still down, knocked out, and covered in shit. I asked Biggie what ever happened to Curt, because no one ever saw him after that day. After everyone left, Biggie was really gonna call the ambulance, but Curt all of a sudden woke up, wiped the poop off his face, and walked out without a word. He just walked away, never to be seen again. Good riddance. One less bully in New Jersey.

Back at the orphanage I was treated to a hero's welcome by everyone but Sister Satan, who thought wrestling was for homosexuals.

"You know wrestling is for homosexuals? And homosexuality is a sin," she would always yammer.

At this time, I was unsure of what *homosexual* really meant, but I knew you didn't want to be it. If you were, you could only hang out with them, whoever the hell homosexuals were.

"Jesus always hung out with men," I said.

She slapped me with all her might. I knew where all her buttons were and was gonna push them until they broke.

She slapped me once again. You can say a lot of bad things about Sister Satan, but she was quick to pull the trigger and had no fear of slapping kids around. Her slaps were quick little stingers, but the more you got, the more immune to them you became.

"Didn't one of his friends get him killed on the big wooden cross thing or something because he was heartbroken? " I said.

The other nuns laughed at my stupidity and jokes. Sister Satan, not so much. She had two nuns hold me down so she could whoop me with the paddle. She gave it her all and whooped my butt until it was bleeding, but that didn't faze me at all because I was the ACW Intercontinental Champion. I didn't have time to cry about getting beat by women. I didn't even have time to honor them with a look of pain.

Pro wrestling has always been there for me. It was my fantasy world. It was the place I could escape to and forget all of my problems and worries. I had my pro wrestling like Sister Satan had her Bible.

I carried that title around with me like Dinker carried around Mr. Coco Blacky. Biggie and the ACW crew bugged me every day to defend my title, calling me a coward and a paper champion. I just kept saying I had thirty days—even when I had way less than thirty days—then I'd kiss the title belt.

Muscle Car always spewed off about contracts and regulations.

There were no contracts though! There wasn't even anything on paper! It was Muscle Car's overactive imagination. The same overactive imagination that led him to poop in a kid's mouth!

By the time day twenty-eight came rolling around, someone had ratted out Vinnie for robbing houses. Suspiciously enough, I was with him for a few of those jobs. Everyone thought I had ratted him out, but I ain't no rat.

I know what you're thinking, but I ain't no rat! So shut your mouth!

Finally, the dreaded Day Thirty came. Back in the ACW Arena, a.k.a. Biggie's family's shop basement, I was ready. But apparently, Vinnie wasn't as ready, because he didn't even show. To nobody's surprise, he was preoccupied in a place I like to call jail, but was really only a juvenile detention center. What's the difference, though? It's jail for kids.

Everyone was booing me. Can you believe they booed the IC champ? How dare they! They were all volunteering to beat me up, just wanting to pull that precious title from me. I was easy pickin's.

"Fight me!" the kids cried over and over. I just answered no every single time.

People were losing their minds with anger.

"I had a contract to fight Vinnie. He is not here, so I win! See you in another thirty!" Some short fat kid, who I'd never seen before, called me a rat bastard.

The place was coming unglued. They started shoving me. I had to figure something out or I was going to get my ass handed to me by everyone in that room. I had to think on my feet.

I spoke loud and proud. "I will wrestle Biggie! Title versus title in thirty days. Warrior versus Hogan style!"

What the hell was I thinking? I will tell you. I was thinking of getting out of that damn basement alive that day, and nothing more.

As soon as the words left my mouth the decision seemed unanimous.

Everyone there accepted the terms: Biggie, Muscle Car, even Bucky—who I thought had my back. Bucky went so far as to sell tickets to my funeral. Seriously, Lucky's Funeral, that was the name of the match. I know it was in good fun, but it didn't help my confidence at all.

I hoped they would forget about it. I even stopped carrying my title around town. Out of sight, out of mind. Right?

Wrong. They didn't forget about it. No one forgot about it. There were handmade posters all around town. I pulled them down when no one was looking, but it was no use. They were back by the time I walked by again the next day.

Peewee tried to talk me out of it.

"Are you nuts? What were you thinking? Biggie is going to destroy you. He weighs in at nine hundred pounds and is over twenty feet tall."

Peewee exaggerated a bit.

"I have to get out of there with my title," I said.

"It is a piece of bent aluminum with friggin' sparkles! Forget about it!"

Except, Peewee said it like they do in those mafia

movies with the guy who was in *Home Alone*: "fuggetabbadit!"

"Forget about it? Forget about it?! Is the Stanley Cup just a cup?!"

"What?"

Peewee was stumped, and I don't know if it was from my situation or the Stanley Cup rhetorical question. He didn't wanna see his older brother, Lucky, get beat down in front of the rich kids. He snapped his fingers, which is what he always did when an idea hit him.

"Take the high road and just give them back their title."

Some idea. Wouldn't that have been the same as "fuggetingabbadit"?

"Only cowards take the high road," I said.

Peewee shook his head. His mouth was wide open, but he wasn't saying anything. "Peewee, I have to do this. I could be the world champion of something."

"And what will that get you?"

"Respect, honor, and most importantly, more pudding cups in the cafeteria. The proof is in the pudding." I knew I was using Bucky's line in the wrong context, but either Peewee didn't care or didn't notice.

The day of the fight, the ACW Arena was packed. They sold as many tickets as they could, which I never saw a penny of. They sold tickets to all of the Jens in town. Too bad Dinker wasn't there though. She said she didn't wanna pay to watch me get my butt kicked when she could see it any other day for free.

I had Peewee as my corner man. Everyone was cheering for Biggie. The orphans, earlier in the day, said they wanted me to win, but when they were reminded of how much larger Biggie was, they jumped on his bandwagon. I wonder if David had this problem with Goliath?

Muscle Car rang the bell, or shook the can if you wanna be all technical about it, and the place went crazy. I went straight in and swung at Biggie with all my might. His defense moves were amazing. Nothing in the world is more humbling than fighting a guy you can't even hit, especially when you take into account his size. Not only was Biggie bigger, he was also quicker and a better boxer. I was boned.

I missed with five shots in a row. He hit me with one of his thunder slaps. It was instant pain. Sister Satan had nothing on Biggie's slaps. Tears instantly burst out of my eyes. The stinging was so bad, and now I couldn't even see. I didn't know if Biggie was gonna do me the favor of not completely messing up my face, so I ducked to save what little of my good looks I had then.

Head down, I got right into his crotch area. He got me up into a pile driver. A pile driver is when your opponent lifts you upside down and then spikes your head into a mat.

The pros protect each other, and they still get killed sometimes!

We were not pros and we didn't even have so much as indoor carpeting in that nasty, cramped basement.

Looking back, I don't even know how I managed to survive that. You always see crazy stuff on *America's Funniest Home Videos*, with these little toddlers being charged at by goats or something, or knocked in the head with footballs or whatever. They just roll with it and walk away giggling. I think we're most resilient in our youth.

I only remember my sense of balance going haywire before getting conked. Hell, it took me a few seconds before I even realized what Biggie had just done. I looked to Muscle Car to make sure he still had his pants on. I hoped to God no one hated me enough to poop in my mouth if I got KO'd or became "indisposed."

Jeez, all that violence and getting pooped in the

mouth—but only second to me losing the title.

I tapped out immediately. I tried to scream that I quit, but nothing came out. Later, everyone would give me credit for not tapping out, but the truth is, no one saw me do it. I never felt such a sharp pain before. I just remember repeating to myself, "Wiggle your toes." I heard it in some movie before.

The ref, who *wasn't* Bucky that day, counted to three. I didn't move. I couldn't. He could have counted to a million and I wouldn't have kicked out. Biggie held up both titles and the fans went berserk. It was so loud. I missed when they rooted for me. The top of my head felt wet.

I looked over to Peewee. Peewee was collecting money.

My own brother and corner man, Peewee, had bet against me. I couldn't stay mad at him, because he used the money to buy me, Dinker, and himself dinner at White House Subs. White House in Atlantic City has the best subs on the planet and that's just science.

I lay in the ring, only because I really couldn't do anything else.

"Wiggle your toes," I said, but I couldn't feel them to know if I was wiggling them or not.

Peewee was too busy counting his money to bother with me. The only one to come to my aid was Korean Jen. No surprise she was there. After all, it was her house too. And what would you know? She asked me if I could move my toes.

"I think."

"You want to get up?"

"No, not yet."

"You need anything?"

"Just make sure Muscle Car doesn't try to poop in my mouth."

CHAPTER 4
The New & Improved Lucky the Orphan


When I first told Dinker and Peewee about our new cousin, Korean Jen, they got angry. Dinker started to look for a bat but Peewee calmed her down, thank God. Dinker eventually broke and agreed on Korean Jen being our new cousin, only after we told her that cousins must give us free candy from their parents' shop and free Korean barbecue. Nothing is better than Korean BBQ. Korean BBQ is so good, I would kill a man for it.

Once Korean Jen was sworn in, she became—officially—a part of the family. Her brother, Biggie, was also in on it and became our cousin too. Korean Jen's parents thought it was annoying, but cute. Peewee was excited to hang with Biggie and Korean Jen. There wasn't much change in Dinker, she was still her same grumpy self.

The best part about being cousins with Jen was that we had access to a Nintendo as long as we didn't steal or touch anything. Jen's house was amazingly clean and everything was always perfectly set. I remember Korean Jen's mom having this collection of miniature carousels. It was creepy, yet beautiful. Korean Jen's dad had a huge collection of computer games. I thought to myself, he must have every game ever. Korean Jen's parents were so cool.

I told Korean Jen's mother she had nothing to worry

about because I was the new and improved Lucky, which meant no more stealing—or at least not until after Christmas. She giggled at my dumb comment. It made me feel great that I could make someone as hot as Korean Jen's mom laugh.

I had apologized to Sister Satan and told her about my plan. She just snarled and told me she'd believe it when she saw it. I told her as a joke to, "Have faith, Sister. Have faith." Sister Satan's negativity only motivated me more to prove her wrong. I went to church every Sunday, was well behaved, and pretended to listen and pray just to rub it in her face.

I got all my teachers apples, studied more, even volunteered to stay after class to clean the blackboards and erasers. My grades improved, but I had to sneak the books out of the school and make sure no one saw me studying, or I would have got a serious ass whooping.

A wise old man once told me being poor in New Jersey is like being a crab in a bucket. Everyone climbs on each other to get ahead, and as soon as one makes it to the top, the others just drag it back down so no one can get out of the bucket.

If any of the other orphans saw me taking home books to study, they would have beat me down. In their eyes they saw that as you thinking you were too good to be one of them. New Jersey is called the Garden State, but it really should be called the Misery Loves Company State.

I even helped the nuns with their garden, laundry, and other chores. Doing laundry at the orphanage taught me one thing: orphans really need to be taught how to wipe their asses properly. All the nuns treated me so nice, except Sister Satan, who went so far as to tempt me to be evil. She was my talking snake. She wanted to see me fail.

One time I came running into the orphanage with a bucket of clean sheets—or at least as clean as they were going to get, some of those yellow stains were permanent—when a couple of older orphans who were up to no good tripped me. I fell flat on my face and the sheets went sliding across the floor.

My two new cousins were with Peewee and Dinker and saw me when I bit the dust. They came running to my aid.

Dinker screamed, "What the hell, guys?"

My family was surrounded by the other orphans, who were ready to throw down. I stood up and wiped some blood from my cut lip.

I tried to calm everyone down. "Whoa! What's going on, guys?"

King Bully Dennis calmed his side down. Dennis was the toughest kid in all of New Jersey. He was the leader of the older orphans and had never lost a fight. If Dennis wanted to fight you, it would only take one punch to knock you out cold. He was your typical '80s New Jersey bad boy; he had shoulder-length hair, always wore shades, and had a denim or leather jacket depending on what he had recently taken by force.

Today he was wearing a Bon Jovi denim jacket. He always had a pack of cigarettes, but no one knew if he really smoked or not. He was cool in every way. Rumor also had it that he had sex with the younger pretty nuns. No one knew what sex was at that time and no one knew anyone who smoked, but we all assumed Dennis did both because he was way more mature than the rest of us.

The last thing anyone wanted was to be on Dennis's bad side. I didn't want my family getting beat up by the others, and above all, I didn't wanna ruin my deal with Santa.

Dennis poked me in the chest and I almost wet myself in fear. It's funny, no matter how brave you are, someone can zap all your courage out like it was nothing. Dennis, in his way-too-deep-to-be-a-kid's voice said, "Lucky, you trying to make us look bad?"

"Who, me? Why would I do that?" It was like I was trying to squeeze my words through a straw.

"Think about it, Dennis. It's me, Lucky."

A kid named Jake stepped forward. He was a bit

younger than Dennis, but for some reason looked like a forty-year-old construction worker. He chimed in, "More like Lucky-rican the ass-kisser!"

Everyone shared a laugh at my expense.

I snapped back, "Lucky-rican? I'm not even brown!"

Korean Jen and Biggie tried really hard not to show how pissed off they were. No one from Dennis's side said anything, so I kept talking.

"And about the ass-kisser part . . . Come on, guys, you know me. I'm Lucky for Christ's sake. I'm no ass-kisser."

Dennis settled his back against the wall, eyeing me over in judgement. If I didn't smooth-talk myself out of this one, I would be one more name to add to his KO record book.

Jake interrupted me.

"If you're not a butt-kisser then what's up with doing all the nuns' work for them?"

Jake was tough but dumb. Two things about Jake: he never wore shoes and he would poop in the middle of the street. Whenever someone would ask him about why he pooped in the street he would say that people would think it's dog poop. But no one ever thought it was dog poop. Human feces have a very distinct smell and look if you ask me.

Some chunky kid with a screechy voice in the back rang in after Jake with a, "And I saw him helping out teachers at the school too!"

God, that voice. I could swear it was the same kid who called me a rat bastard at that wrestling match. What gives?

I raised my voice so everyone could hear me. "Okay. Okay. Okay. Listen up, I'm not trying to make anyone look bad. I'd never do that." All eyes were on me as I looked around.

"It's all part of the plan . . ." I said with a smirk. I had to act cocky. I had to act like I knew something that they didn't.

Jake still looked upset, but I could hear that he was

now curious.

"What plan?"

"A plan to get us a Nintendo."

Everyone laughed. They believed that they would never see a Nintendo in their lifetime at the orphanage.

But I knew I had my foot in their door. As I expected, Jake continued.

"You and your Nintendo dreams. We ain't gonna get any Nintendo, you chump!"

"But I have a *plan*!" I said, dropping the P-word again.

"Plan" is such a sophisticated word. Plans are elaborate and thought-out. If I had told them from the get-go I was gonna get us a Nintendo they would have called BS and socked me one in the gut. But if you use the P-word it makes everything sound so secret and smart. You not only know what you want, but have thought out a method to get it. It told them that I knew something that they didn't.

"Start talking, Lucky," Jake said.

"I'm going to be good all year, and then on Christmas, we will have a Nintendo! Done and done!"

"That doesn't work. That's not even a plan."

"Yes, it will, and yes, it is. We always get horrible gifts every year because we are horrible people. We are always on the naughty list. Peewee is a good kid. He tries to be rotten like us, but deep down inside he is nice."

The orphans seemed unsure. Dennis started cracking his knuckles. I was running out of time. Where was that sweet-talker Bucky when you needed him? I had to think on my feet.

"Peewee, what did you ask for Christmas?"

Peewee softly answered, "A Fast Eddie Hot Wheels."

"And what did you get?"

"A Fast Eddie Hot Wheels."

"See? It's science. If we're good, Santa brings us what we ask for. Peewee was just too dumb to ask for a bigger gift."

There was some unsure mumbling. I had made a sturdy

argument, but it still needed beefing up.

"It's science, I'm telling you! Did I ever let you down before? I'm the reason the Philly Fanatic came to our Thanksgiving party! I'm the reason we all have Starter jackets. When I have a plan it benefits all of us."

I had nothing left. I prayed that Dennis or Jake bought it. If I managed to win at least one over he could convince the other. Dennis started to walk towards me.

I blurted out, "I guarantee you, I will get us a Nintendo by Christmas Day!" Dennis stopped and put a funny look on his face.

Dennis said, "You guarantee us a Nintendo by Christmas?"

I was in too deep and had started spouting off the empty promise of a Nintendo like I was some fast-talking Jersey politician.

"I guarantee we will have a Nintendo by Christmas Day. I freaking guarantee it!"

I must have said the word *guarantee* like forty times, and like good card-carrying party voters, they bought it.

Dennis got real close and whispered in my ear. "If you don't deliver us a Nintendo, I will have to kill you, dude."

I let out a deep breath and then whispered back, "I know."

Dennis's attitude changed instantly. He raised my hand as if I'd won a boxing—or wrestling—match and started a Nintendo chant. All the kids were chanting "Nintendo!"

I had won them over. They carried me around like I'd just won the Super Bowl, or Stanley Cup. This was more recognition than I'd had being an ACW Intercontinental Champion. Some kids, who didn't even know what the hell was going on, followed my lead. The empty promise I had just made had lifted everyone's spirits. Everything in the world would be okay now. I just had to stick to the plan and Santa would do the rest.

# CHAPTER 5
## Peewee Accomplishes His Mission

As far as North Easterners go, New Jersey usually gets to be the butt of everyone's jokes, but one thing about New Jersey that we can take pride in is that we have four seasons. And on one particular day, it was unusually cool for summer.

Me and Biggie were out tossing "the ole pigskin" that day. Biggie had a good arm and was about three telephone poles away. That was pushing it for me. I'm not a great athlete, but I am always proud of the fact that I never fumbled any of Biggie's long bomb throws.

"C'mon Lucky, here's a long one!" he'd say. "They're all long ones!"

Biggie'd always ask, "You know why they call this a pigskin?"

"Because it's made out of a pig's skin, duh!"

Dinker was warming up to Korean Jen just fine. They became super close cousins and were doing everything together. Despite Korean Jen being our cousin, she played more of a big sister role. This was good, because Dinker really needed that in her life back then. It was funny to me that, even though she was doing teenage-girl-type stuff, she still carried around Mr. Blacky everywhere. As for me and Korean Jen, we were cool as cousins, but nowhere near as close as we were before. I just kept asking myself the same question: Why in the hell did I say no to her? It didn't seem to bother her as much as it bothered me.

Peewee was riding Biggie's bike. He was trying to accomplish his mission of riding it with no hands. Since the beginning of the year, Peewee would pedal full speed with one hand and work up the courage to let go. He got a handmade wooden ramp from a local construction yard and everything. He would jump it, and when he was airborne he'd scream, "Cowabunga!"

I always wanted Biggie's bike. It was bright yellow with no logos or stickers of any kind. Instead of the usual silver spokes, his wheels were purple with three big flat metal spokes. I thought they looked more like the rims for a car than for a bike. Looking back now, they looked nothing like car rims. Biggie could have had any bike he wanted, him being a rich kid and all, but he had one that was built and painted by his father.

I asked him once why he didn't want one of the expensive ones, and he just responded with, "Because, this bike is unique, like me." I just nodded. I didn't really know what the word "unique" meant back then, but when I looked it up later, I ended up nodding again. Biggie was definitely unique.

Me and Biggie became super close cousins over the summer. He was my best friend growing up. He liked all the same things I liked: pro wrestling, comic books, and of course, Nintendo. Biggie was talented at everything he did, and that's what made him so cool. He was the best athlete on our block and could kick anyone's butt at Nintendo, in any game. He got good grades, could draw almost anything, and he could write the most amazing stories ever.

I wish he was still here—maybe he could give me tips on writing this story. Biggie could write a good story. He once wrote this story about a girl who fell in love at Six Flags with a boy she met in line for Rolling Thunder—or maybe it was the Great American Scream Machine. I really can't remember now. Anyways, she kept going back to go on dates with him because he could never leave the park because he was a ghost or something. From this, she learned a valuable lesson about not being a slut . . . or something. Yeah, I know it doesn't sound that good when I tell it, but when Biggie told it, it was amazing.

Once, Biggie got a gift certificate as a prize for winning a writing contest at school with that story. It was worth a few hundred dollars. With it, he bought almost all of the Garfield collections and a ton of Stephen King books. He'd let me borrow them, but only one at a time.

I was an angry kid, and most of my childhood was horrible in my eyes. I know whenever I say that I've had hard times to people, a lot of them just try to one-up me with their own sob story about their dog running away or something. I don't know if they're trying to make me feel better or what. If someone comes to tell me that their daddy used to touch them or something, I'm not going to reply with, "Well, I didn't have any parents." Seriously, what gives?

I may have hated my own childhood, but Peewee—even though he had most of the same experiences—loved his. I know this because he tells me how much he loved his childhood. I wish I didn't have so much hate in my heart and could be more like Peewee. No matter how crappy life was, Peewee always saw some good in it.

The only place where I was ever happy was at Six Flags Great Adventure, and thanks to our new cousins, we went there at least once a week in the summer.

To this day, no matter how much life stresses me out, if I go to an amusement park I am happy and can think clearly. It doesn't matter your age, dreams come alive at theme parks. As mentioned earlier in this memoir, autobiography, whatever the hell you wanna call it, I always dreamed I would be important to the world somehow. You know? Not only be rich and famous, but do something great for the world.

On one of our trips to Six Flags Great Adventure the park was nearly empty and we could just run up to any roller coaster with no wait. It was awesome. It felt like the park was only open to serve us. Peewee was watching the high-dive show for the fourth time that day, and Korean Jen and Dinker had gone off to Bugs Bunny Land to get fake Tweety Bird tattoos or whatever it is girls do at theme parks. So it was just me and Biggie. Also, Korean Jen looked amazing in the bikini she was wearing that day—I don't know what that has to do with the story, but I feel it has to be mentioned.

Me and Biggie were gonna ride Rolling Thunder for the tenth time in a row and we were running through the maze of bars that usually guides the line of people. I guess we could have just ducked under all the bars, but for some reason, we were just really excited. I can remember how excited I was because my voice was squeaking like crazy that day.

"Can you believe it? Rolling Thunder ten times in a row!"

An older kid with his girlfriend overheard me and mocked my voice. It was enough of an embarrassment to keep me from running. I put my head down and walked.

I couldn't beat him up because of how much older and bigger he was, and I  couldn't make fun of his date because she was smoking hot. Plus, I didn't even have a date. Worst part was that the coolest guy I knew, Biggie, had just seen me get punked out.

But Biggie avenged me by making fun of the older kid for picking on me. He said to the kid that his girlfriend was way too good for him.

"A girl like you must be really impressed by a guy who can ruin a kid's day," he said. "You actually like this D-bag?"

She said *no*, and then started fighting with her boyfriend, or whatever he was. That D-bag was a real jerk for ruining my day, and when Biggie punked him, the kid did nothing. I was so happy that kid and his girlfriend were fighting. When we came around, the D-bag's girlfriend made him apologize to me.

Now, I could have taken the high road, but that wasn't my style. I told him, "No, thank you, I learned a real valuable lesson today."

Biggie seemed surprised by my remark. The D-bag bully asked me, "Really?"

"Yeah, because when I'm older I'll get to date a girl as pretty as yours," I winked at his date. "Because I won't be an asshat bully. Thanks."

The D-bag bully was embarrassed he couldn't do anything because of his girlfriend, and also Biggie would've smashed him.

The D-bag's girlfriend hung out with me and Biggie in the empty line of Rolling Thunder. I can't remember her name for the life of me, but I remember us arguing who was the best Winnie the Pooh character: Eeyore or Piglet. I'm really surprised Tigger never came up.

As me and Biggie were playing catch that day in the street, I couldn't help but remember that day at Six Flags. That was the first time in my life someone had my back! And it felt amazing. Biggie was the coolest kid I knew and I got to have him as a cousin, best friend, but above all, my hero.

Oh, damn! Peewee does it! No hands! And he had on the biggest smile in the world. I try not to be a jealous person, but at that moment, I was so jealous Peewee accomplished his mission before I accomplished my mission of getting a Nintendo. I shouldn't have been that angry, but I was. I tried to play it off by giving him some big brother advice. "Be safe, Peewee! Don't get hurt, bud."

He smirked. "Don't worry, I can do it. Can you?"

If I had the sense to call Peewee a smug little bastard back then, I would've. Biggie called him an A-hole. Peewee raced up the street to try it again. Biggie started poking the bear by turning to me and saying, "Lucky, you want to be a

Marine, a Marine sniper, and you're going to take that attitude from Peewee?"

"Ahh . . .What can I do?"

Biggie looked disappointed. "You don't have the killer instinct to be a Marine," he said.

Peewee was flying down the street with no hands, mocking me for not being able to do something he could. He was on top of the world, and for him, that meant that being humble was thrown out the window.

I was so angry, and Biggie was pushing all the right buttons. As soon as Peewee was lined up to me, without any hesitation I threw the football. I managed to hit the front tire of Biggie's bike. It was the most perfect throw I ever achieved. Enough to make Joe Montana blush with envy.

Biggie's bike, with Peewee on it, flipped. Peewee did a face-plant on the street. It all happened so fast. The world went silent for me. For a few seconds, I thought Peewee was dead. Then Peewee started screaming in pain.

Biggie was so shocked that he just ran away, leaving his unique bike and pigskin behind. My hero, Biggie, flew the coop that day, but I'll still give him credit, because it was the only time I'd ever seen him run away from anything.

I regret to say this, but in those few moments of silence, I felt so good to have hurt Peewee. It took me a few seconds to realize how hurt he really was, and also how screwed-up I was to have done that. You know how they always say you can't change the past? Well, out of all the stuff they always say, that one is actually true. You really *can't* change the past. You'd be stupid to even try.

# CHAPTER 6
## Peewee's Scar


Sadly, what broke me from being a monster wasn't how much I cared for my little brother, but how Santa could find out. That would mean no Nintendo for Christmas; and no Nintendo meant Dennis was going to kill me.

I ran for Peewee to help him up. He held back his tears, but couldn't stop the blood and snot from pouring out of his face. Peewee had never hated or said he hated anything the whole time I had known him, but now Peewee just kept repeating how much he hated me. He had blood coming out of his mouth and nose, and a huge gash above his left eye. His elbows and knees were scraped up pretty bad. I had never seen someone so bloody and beat-up before. It was bad. It was real bad.

I held my little brother up and helped him back to the orphanage. He may have hated me, but he still wasn't above saying he needed my help. I tried to explain that I only did it to teach him a lesson. Kinda like tough love, I guess. Just to keep him safe.

He wasn't buying it for one second. The closer we got to the orphanage, the more desperate I got. I begged him not to tell anyone. It was time to pull out my bargaining chips.

"Remember when you pissed behind the shed, Peewee? Remember?"

I was referring to one of the worst beatings that me and Peewee got, the year before when we were playing in the backyard and had to use the restroom. I had suggested that we pee outside, because for some reason, I've always got a kick outta peeing outside. Especially at night. Nothing beats looking up at the night sky while you're emptying your bladder. Call me nuts, but one of the bigger accomplishments in my life is that I have peed outside on every continent—but I guess that's a story for another time.

Anyway, backyard: Peewee was walking inside to use the toilet. I grabbed his shoulder and convinced him it would take way too long to go inside and come back out, and we were in the middle of an intense game of boxball. I pointed to the shed and smiled. Peewee looked at the shed and then looked at the door leading inside. I swear you could hear him thinking it over. Technically, it was the same distance and really wouldn't have taken any longer. I guess I was just being difficult. Peewee finally shrugged and followed me to the shed as the other kids screamed for us to hurry so we could continue the game.

Me and Peewee darted behind the shed. We must have drunk too much grape-flavored Kool-Aid because we peed for what seemed to a kid like forever. It was like the aliens were stealing time again. Peewee giggled and said he'd never gone that long before. We hadn't even gotten to pull our pants back up when Sister Satan grabbed us by the ears and dragged us back inside. Our wieners were out and hanging in the breeze for everyone to see.

Sister Satan threw us face down on the bed with our bare bottoms to the sky. She nodded at the other nuns and they held us down. I'd like to think that the other sisters were against this and that S.S. was forcing them to hold us down, but to tell you the truth, all those sickos probably loved it.

S.S. beat us silly. Our butts were covered in these splotchy red freckles. S.S. kept ranting and raving about our sins, and about how we should know better, and also something about praying the gay away. I remember thinking to myself that God must hate everyone that takes a wizz outside. I looked into Peewee's eyes and saw this look on his face like he was dead inside too.

I was about to cry from the pain, but then Peewee uttered the words that would eventually see me through many a hard time: "We are better than them."

S.S. and the other nuns finally stopped beating us to tell us we should wait till we're older to love like that—but with a woman because it was God's way. And for a few years after, Peewee thought that meant that God wanted him to pee with girls. Seeing that dead look on Peewee's face, even after his words of encouragement, I had to help him. I told S.S. that going behind the shed was all my idea. S.S. asked Peewee if it was true. He nodded, so they let him go. Peewee never talked about that day ever again, no matter how many kids asked or made fun of him.

The nuns beat me for a little while longer, but it didn't seem to hurt as much anymore. I just kept repeating to myself, "I am better than you."

I was getting desperate and now harping on Peewee.

"Remember the shed? Remember how bad Sister Satan beat us, Peewee?"

I guess that it didn't faze him. I couldn't believe that he was seriously thinking about ratting me out to Sister Satan.

I was desperate.

I harped on him again.

"What about Santa and the Nintendo?"

Peewee didn't curse that much back then, which only made me more surprised because he was shouting too.

"DAMN THE NINTENDO!" he said.

I dropped him. I had to. Peewee fell like a bloody sack of potatoes. I was so angry I kicked him. This was not one of my proudest moments, but I'm not gonna lie and say that it didn't feel good, for me that is . . .

"Watcha sayin'?" I grumbled.

Peewee stayed down, but covered up. I just kept kicking him. "Say it again!"

Kick.

"I dare you." Kick.

"All we want is a Nintendo!" Kick.

I corrected myself. "I need this Nintendo!" Kick, and by that point, I was screaming. "I WILL GET A NINTENDO!"

I kept kicking him until Dennis and a few others ran over and pulled me away.

Dennis, as the leader/King Bully of The Orphans, asked what was going on in his deep manly voice. Dennis's minions picked up the bloody and beaten Peewee from the ground.

Peewee tried to tell Dennis what happened, but was so out of it with so much blood and spit coming out of his mouth that all we could hear were the words "Lucky," "Biggie," "football," "bike," and "crash."

I just pointed at Peewee and yelled, "He is going to rat me out, and then we won't get a Nintendo."

No one likes a rat. Orphans especially don't like rats. But since no one really knew what me and Peewee were talking about, Dennis just held his hand in the air and took over everything like he always did.

Dennis commanded, "Listen up. This is what is going to happen. No one is ratting on anyone." He lightly grabbed Peewee's chin and looked into his eyes like he was some kinda dog. "I will make sure Lucky will pay for this, but you will not ruin us getting a Nintendo. Do you understand?"

Peewee managed a nod before going limp. I said, "Santa can never know!"

Dennis ignored me, and pointed at Pewee and the other

orphans. "Take him around back and patch him up. Make sure Sister Satan doesn't see a thing."

They dragged Peewee around back and taped him up using old rags and duct tape. Poor kid needed stitches and all they did was keep replacing the duct tape for him over and over. I'll never forgive myself for giving him those scars.

Once everyone was gone, Dennis put his arm around me and asked, "Head or gut?"

"Huh?"

I knew what he was talking about, I was just trying to stall. "C'mon, Lucky, head or gut?"

"Gut."

I swear Dennis swung his fist at my gut before I even answered. Maybe he decided before I did. I know this because I didn't really say the word *gut*—it more or less came out with a burst of air as the wind was being knocked out of me. I have never been punched that hard in my life. I couldn't even breathe in enough to talk. I dropped down into a ball. I even pissed myself a bit.

As I lay there, Dennis got real close to my ear and whispered, "You better get this Nintendo, or I'm going to kill you."

If only Korean Jen was there to nurse me to my feet.

Dennis walked away. I lay on the ground in pain, not able to speak a word, but thinking of how much of a D-bag I was. Like that kid at Six Flags.

The next day, with duct tape over his left eye, Peewee acted as if nothing happened. I think one of Peewee's superpowers is to forgive and forget. Maybe that is his secret to always being happy. I envy him for that.

Peewee would have a scar on his left eyebrow for the rest of his life. I don't know what he thought of it but every time I saw it, it reminded me of how much of an ass I was to him. It also reminded me that I had a killer instinct, and if I could hurt someone I loved this much, imagine what I could do to my enemies.

Me and Peewee never fought ever again after that day. And I never hurt him again, as that scar was a constant symbol of what evils I was capable of.

# CHAPTER 7
## Christmas in July

Sister Satan didn't care enough to wanna know why Peewee was all banged up and had his head taped together with dollar store duct tape. We figured that if she didn't know, maybe Santa was none the wiser either. But we still intended to find out exactly how much Santa actually knew, and we— and by "we" I mean "I"—had an airtight plan.

Dinker overheard us and wanted in on what our mastermind plan was. "So what is it, guys?"

"You're a girl, you won't understand," I said.

Peewee nudged me with his elbow. It was his way of saying, "Tell her, Lucky." Even though he said it too.

I spent the next minute beating around the bush, until Dinker finally screamed, "Just tell me what it is!"

I let her have it. "We're just going to ask him."

She dropped Coco Blacky on the floor and slapped her own forehead. "You guys are morons."

I looked to Peewee, my eyes affirming what I had said before: she's a girl, I told you she wouldn't understand.

I can't believe Dinker called me a moron. I doubt she could think of a better plan. "It's so simple it's genius," I said to her with my cocky smile. I was trying to play off the fact that Dinker, who couldn't even think up a decent name for her black Cabbage Patch Kids, just insulted me.

Dinker's mouth was hanging open a little bit. "We're

not getting no damn Nintendo," she flatly said, then walked away cursing to herself.

Peewee grabbed Mr. Blacky off the floor before any of the other girls could steal him. Granted, everyone busted his balls for having a girl's toy, but he didn't care. He just didn't want Coco Blacky to be stolen because he knew how happy that doll made Dinker feel.

Well, the entire plan was hanging on the fact that Santa was coming to visit the orphanage that day. Everyone was cheerful and on their best behavior. I think every sentence spoken that day had something to do with Santa. The older kids were patting me on the back and giving me words of encouragement that entire day. Everyone there, no matter their age, was looking forward to that Nintendo that I promised.

We all gathered in the one big room downstairs. It was packed and super hot. We heard bells jingling and we went nuts. We were cheering so loud. A few seconds later, Santa strode in and the place erupted like he was the second coming of Christ—or would it be the third coming? I mean, wasn't Easter his second coming?

Santa gave off a "Ho-ho-ho!" and we just about lost our minds. Before he sat down he gave a small speech about how we were so special and that he had to visit us first or some junk like that. I really didn't care about anything he said. I had my mission. I had to find out about what he knew.

My eyes shot over to Dinker. I could tell she was just eating it up. She had tears of joy and was hugging Mr. Blacky tight. She whispered into his ear. I couldn't hear her over the other kids, but I saw her lips move to say the word "special."

Santa made a joke about one of his reindeer wanting a carrot, which I thought was stupid.

Some of the other kids laughed, but it wasn't real laughter. It was pity laughter. Santa had the power to revoke our presents and we all knew this, so some of us figured we'd better humor the guy. It's amazing how perceptive kids can be sometimes.

Santa asked who wanted to go first. I shot my arm in the air and shouted, "Me!" I made sure to put a please at the end, but I would have gone first anyway because everyone was chanting my name. "Lu-cky! Lu-cky! Lu-cky!"

When I die, I hope to get to live that moment over at least one more time. There is no better feeling than hearing people chanting your name and rooting for you. I mean, if that isn't nice, I don't know what is.

Santa chuckled.  "I guess Lucky is first then."

I ran up to Santa and jumped into his lap. I landed with a thud, which made him cringe for a split second, then he went back to his jolly old self.

"Ho-ho-ho! Lucky! That's a nice name!" Santa's breath hit me in the face. He smelled like Father O'Touches-a-lot and dry cleaning. "Well, Lucky, what do *you* want for Christmas?"

Stop for a sec. Lemme fill you in on Father O'touches-a-lot. He was the priest/boss that was in charge of the orphanage and was like the nuns' manager or something. We didn't see him often, but that man could hug for hours. Just ask Dinker. I don't remember what his real name was, but he was Irish so it really was "O'(Something)."

Anyway, back to Santa.

"You know everything, right?" I asked Santa. There was a hush over the room.

Santa let out a little chuckle, then spoke loudly for all to hear. "Of course I do, I'm Santa after all!" He had the whole room in the palm of his hand.

"So you won't mind if I ask you a few questions then?"

Santa had a weird expression on his face, but let out another "Ho-ho-ho!" I guess that meant yes.

"So yeah, like, do you know? About how Peewee got hurt?"

Everyone leaned in. It was like up till then, no answer

was ever as important as what Santa was gonna say next. There was a long pause. Some kids looked angrily to Peewee, who was still patched up with tape.

"Ah yes, ho-ho-ho! Peewee . . . About Peewee. Now, where is he? He's here, right?"

Everyone pointed to Peewee, but they didn't really need to. Peewee was still recovering from his injuries. Having duct tape on his head, he stuck out like a sore thumb. The orphans were ready to pounce on him at a moment's notice if he slipped up. If anyone was in the hot seat that day, it wasn't me, it was Peewee.

"Ah! There you are, Peewee. I don't know how I could have missed you . . ." Santa's eye twitched as he looked at Peewee. "And are you okay, Peewee?" You'd swear Santa never saw a kid duct-taped up before.

I am sure that all the kids turning to look at Peewee were making threatening faces or mouthing the words "I will kill you" at that point, and all Santa could see was the back of their heads.

"I'm okay," Peewee answered.

"That must have hurt, huh?" Santa said. "Did you cry?"

What the hell was he asking all these questions for? Didn't he know all this stuff already? Peewee was being very careful with his answers. To think, all Peewee wanted was to see Santa; what he got was the Inquisition.

"It was my fault, sir." Peewee said. "I shouldn't have been riding no-handed."

Santa smiled, and for some completely unrelated reason, at that moment I realized that "Santa" and "Satan" are almost the same thing but just with the last three letters switched around.

"Yes . . ." Santa said. He was pausing an awful lot when he spoke. "That sure was a nasty fall off your bike."

The room was quiet and I realized how hot it was becoming. With all the sweat running off his face, Santa looked like he was gonna melt. Not only that, he started smelling like what he was: a fat and hairy man in a winter coat in the middle of July.

"It was all my fault, sir," Peewee said.

"Let's be more careful next time. It's a good thing you have a friend like Lucky to watch out for you."

Everyone cheered. It was as if the New Jersey Devils had just won the Stanley Cup—Jeez, how many times am I gonna reference the Stanley Cup in here? Santa looked so confused. Santa was a sucker.

"God bless you, Santa," I said with a smile.

Santa gave an even bigger smile. Everyone in the room smiled back, and Peewee was finally out of the hot seat.

"Well, what do you want for Christmas, Lucky?"

I hopped off Santa's lap, spread my arms out, and yelled, "I want a Nintendo for all of us!"

The kids cheered and started chanting "NIN-TEN-DO. NIN-TEN-DO. NIN-TEN-DO." Santa looked to the back of the room at Sister Satan.

I plopped back down on Santa's lap with the force of "Macho Man" Randy Savage's elbow drop, and looked up into his eyes like I was a dirty and hungry puppy.

"I, sorry, *we*, want a Nintendo."

The chanting stopped. We wouldn't miss what Santa had to say next.

But he was stalling. "A Nintendo? A Nin-ten-do . . . Well, Lucky. My elves can't make Nintendos. Nintendos are also expensive."

"But Pube got a Nintendo from you last year!" I said.

"Yeah, what gives?" someone hidden in the crowd said. I could tell it was Dennis. Santa's expression turned not-so-pleasant.

"Pube? Don't use that kind of language! What? You have a friend named Pube? What's wrong with you kids?" Santa had dropped his trademark jolly-talk. Now he sounded like a guy from Jersey, and I don't mean the good part either. He looked to me, then to Sister Satan, and back to me again.

"We have been extra good this year." I waited a second or two and then borrowed the Peewee method of tagging a "sir" on at the end.

"Well . . ." Santa started before getting cut off, by of all people, Sister Satan.

"They have been good," she said.

Everyone was silent with shock, and then went crazy cheering and laughing. That had to be one of the weirdest days for that guy playing Santa and all the nuns. I can't believe S.S. stood up for us, and in front of Santa! I was impressed, and thought to myself, I hope one day I can repay her and make her happy for a moment or two.

Sister Satan tried to yell over the applause. "Get over yourself! I only want you to get that damn Nintendo so you will leave me alone!"

But her message was lost in all the excitement.

"Nintendo?" I asked Santa one more time with a mile-wide smile on my face.

"I'll see what I can do," Santa said.

Sister Satan shot Santa the evil eye. Take a cue, buddy.

Then he spoke his final words. "I will get you a Nintendo if the nuns and elves say you have been good!" Santa said as he looked to Sister Satan.

Everyone went bananas and I jumped into the crowd to be carried away like a rock star or sports hero. We were all so caught up in the excitement we didn't notice Santa slip away after only one Christmas request, mine.

# CHAPTER 8
## Dinker's Dark Secret


After Santa had left, me, Peewee, and Dinker stuck around to help clean up the mess that was left behind. Our spirits were so high. Even Sister Satan was smiling. Our dreams were finally gonna come true, and Santa had just confirmed it for everyone.

As we were cleaning, we heard a car pull up. We ran towards the window to take a peek; it was Father O'Touches-a-lot's white BMW, which was in near-perfect condition.

"Maybe next year you can ask for a car?" Peewee said to me. I think he was serious when he said it too.

Sister Satan's smile disappeared. She demanded we go back to work. Peewee savored the last glimpse of that BMW.

"God must pay well," he said before turning away from the window.

Dinker agreed. "Yeah, God must pay Father O'Touches-a-lot a bunch of money."

I looked to S.S. and asked her, "You work for God, right?"

She sighed a *yes*.

"How come Father O'Touches-a-lot has such a nice car and you have nothing?"

"God works in mysterious ways."

"It just doesn't seem fair," I said. "Maybe you should ask Santa for a BMW."

I suggested this even though I knew S.S. probably wouldn't get one. Not because Santa never got anyone a BMW in the history of Christmas, but because S.S. was a horrible person who would only ever get lumps of coal.

"Sure, Lucky. Sure, maybe I'll ask Santa," she said. Peewee cut in.

"Lucky's gonna ask next year if you don't."

S.S. messed with her coif (nun hat) like she was trying to get to an itch on her head. "Please, Lucky, let's just get everyone to finish this."

Normally, I would've given her a hard time, but she vouched for us in front of Santa. Plus, I think I already did unintentionally give her a hard time asking why she didn't have a BMW.

As we finished cleaning up the place, Father O'Touches-a-lot came in the room and went on and on about how great of a job we did. Sister Satan was trying to hide a dirty look. I don't think she liked him at all. O.T. put his arm around Dinker and pulled her against his hips.

Now, unlike Sister Satan, who was sometimes referred to as S.S., nobody called Father O'Touches-a-Lot O.T. I'm only doing it now because it's easier to type. O.T. loved to talk just about as much as he loved to hug. I didn't mind the talk so much because, at that moment, it was talk about how great we all were. Back then, I was more than happy to receive compliments from someone who drove a BMW. I'm sure Peewee was too. Anyone who had a BMW must have done something right with their life.

O.T. sent us on our way. Dinker tried to follow me and Peewee, but Father O'Touches-a- lot said he needed help with something. He seemed to have a lot of faith in Dinker, because she always had to stay and help him out, even with me and

Peewee offering to help instead. Dinker helped after church, after dinners, and now after cleaning up. I'm not gonna try to hide what was really going on when Dinker went to help O'Touchy. I guess anyone with a brain cell can tell where this whole thing is going anyway. I mean for Christ's sake, the guy's nickname was O'Touches-a-lot! But, at the time, I remember I used to think how lucky Dinker was, getting special treatment all the time.

Me and Peewee left. Dinker went with Father O'Touches-a-lot and helped him with who knows what—well, we do now.

Walking through the orphanage, Peewee and me were made men. Santa didn't know jack, the other orphans loved us, Father O'Touches-a-lot had nothing but good things to say about us, and even S.S. was vouching for us!

Later that night, we watched wrestling. We got to see our hometown hero Bam Bam Bigelow get a win over Barry Horowitz, which led to Bucky telling everyone the New Jersey urban legend of Bam Bam Bigelow. I guess the reason Bam Bam Bigelow had the flame tattoos and outfit was because he saved a bunch of children from a burning house.

Remember, we didn't have the internet back then to fact-check things like that like we do nowadays. Plus, Bucky was a huge bullshitter. He wasn't a compulsive liar or anything, but sometimes he'd lie out of his ass just to see if you were paying attention or not. Worst thing was, it took me years to finally realize it. I'm still trying to sort through all the stuff that he told me. Which were lies and which were true?

After Bam Bam Bigelow, we watched Hulk Hogan battle another New Jersey hometown hero, King Kong Bundy. Urban legend on King Kong Bundy was that he was a local school's math or history teacher, but no one believed it. Imagine, Bam Bam Bigelow saving kids from a fire was more believable than King Kong Bundy teaching.

In the match, King Kong Bundy had Hogan right where he wanted him, but that damn Hulk Hogan started hulking up. And that was when Sister Satan unplugged the TV. Jeering ensued. We all wanted to see King Kong Bundy clobber Hulk Hogan and become champion. We begged S.S. to turn it back on, but she just laughed. She was laughing and getting high off her power trip.

"Bundy can win the title tonight!" I pled.

"Lucky, let me let you in on a little secret about life; it's not fair."

"But King Kong Bundy can win the title tonight!" I pled again.

"You've all been watching these homosexual shows for too long! It is time to go to bed! I'll be damned if I let you impressionable boys watch leotard-wearing men shove each other's crotches in their faces!"

Jeez, I didn't even know what three of the words she just used meant back then. "They're not wearing leo-whatevers! They're wearing tights!" I yelled.

I looked to Peewee and couldn't believe my eyes. He was fighting back tears.

"Why can't you let us stay up?" Peewee said.

"I hate all of you brats. You're all God's mistakes and that is why your parents left you all. I'm stuck taking care of everyone else's mistakes!"

"I thought God didn't make mistakes," I said. I was such a smart aleck. It wasn't to my benefit either. S.S. snapped and started slapping us in the back of the heads, screaming at us like a madwoman until we left for our beds.

"I'll throw this damn TV away is what I'll do!"

That would've sucked, because it would have been hard to play that Nintendo I planned on getting if we didn't have a TV in the common room.

Me and Peewee weren't ready for bed yet. We walked by Dinker's room, arguing over who was the better wrestler,

Ric Flair, or Hulk Hogan. Peewee was a Hulkamaniac and thought Hulk Hogan was too strong for Ric Flair. I was a Ric Flair guy and knew he had more wrestling moves, was the dirtiest player in the game, and had the Four Horsemen as backup at the snap of his fingers. It was a never-ending debate for us.

We stopped arguing when we heard Dinker crying. Peewee was scared and worried. He looked around with panic in his eyes to make sure no one else could hear. I just gave him a look and nodded my head to tell him that I'd take care of it.

I walked into Dinker's room, but she didn't seem to notice. She had her face in her hands.

I put my hand on her shoulder. She was startled and jumped up.

"I wasn't crying. I'm just angry," she said to me as she wiped away her tears. "What happened?" I asked.

"Don't worry, it was nothing."

"Well, it has to be something . . ."

Dinker picked up her brush and started brushing her hair.

"I have dreams. I have goals. I want to be special. You know, every night before bed, my mom would read me Dr. Zeus and tell me how special I was."

"You mean Dr. Seuss? I think you're special. And dreams are good."

Dinker looked to Mr. Coco Blacky sitting on her bed.

"Blacky! Stupid Blacky! How stupid is a white girl carrying a black doll?"

Before I could answer, Dinker reached for a pencil and stabbed Blacky in the head. Then she threw him against the wall by the arm. The arm ripped a bit. Blacky fell on her bed. Dinker jumped on top of Blacky and started punching the doll until its face was flat.

"Blacky is stupid! Dreams are stupid! Goals are stupid! I'm stupid! And you know what else?" she said, still wailing on poor old Blacky. "My grandparents are never coming!"

She snapped out of her violent trance. She was frozen with her fist in the air, but it wouldn't move to hit Blacky anymore. This was the first time Dinker accepted the truth out loud. I think it hit us both like a thousand bricks.

Dinker hopped off the bed and started brushing her hair in the mirror.

"Dreams are stupid," she said before breaking down and starting to cry again. But this time, she really broke down and let it out. It wouldn't've surprised me if the other girls rushed in right then to give Dinker the beating of her lifetime. Dinker, the once strong and stubborn Jersey girl who would beat up anyone just for looking at her funny, was gone. All that was left was a pile of crying goop.

I wanted so bad to help her. All I could think of to blurt out was, "They aren't stupid."

"What do you know? You don't have any dreams of your own."

"Yeah, I do. What about the Nintendo?"

"Oh, brother, I mean real dreams. Not some stupid toy!"

I was so mad at her for calling the Nintendo a "stupid toy." I wanted to scream at her and tell her how awesome it was, but I had to focus and help my sis. But trust me, I made a mental note to bust her balls later about it.

"I do have real dreams, but you might laugh," I said. "I dream to be interviewed on the news, and people listening to what I say will say to themselves what a smart kid I am. I hate that people see me as a dumb person all the time. I may not be the smartest, but I'm smarter than the adults give me credit for."

Earlier that year, a bunch of teachers and Sister Satan

decided it was best for me to go to the SPED classes without even asking me. I might not have been the best student, but I didn't deserve to be in friggin' special ed. I still remember the look Sister Satan gave me when she gave the OK to send me to those classes. She loved it. She knew this would be something to haunt me my whole life.

"I dream to be rich or famous enough for my real parents to know who I am. I'll never go looking for them, but one day I want them to pick up a newspaper or something and know I made something of myself without them. Ya know what I mean?"

Dinker stopped crying and nodded her head for me to go on. This was the first time she got to hear her brother talk about his dreams. I guess it just wasn't my style. I just kept going.

"I dream of my funeral. Kinda sick, right? I dream about a lot of people being there and saying nice things about me and how important I was to them and the world. So yeah, I have dreams too."

Dinker's tears were gone. She looked like her old self again.

I stood up and said, "I would say nice things about you if you died."

"Really?"

"Of course."

Then we hugged each other so tight, like brother and sister, not like how I would want to hug Korean Jen again. We completely forgot who was there to cheer who up. We were both doing our part, and I think that is what family is really about.

After we were both back to ourselves, I read to Dinker her favorite Dr. Seuss book, *The Lorax*. The cover was ripped off and it was missing some pages, but that didn't make the story any less special for her. When I got to her favorite part, she cut me off.

"I care a lot, I really do," she said.

I patted her on the head like if she was a puppy, which seems pretty corny now. "I know," I answered and continued on.

The last few pages of the book were missing, so some nights I would give a sad ending where everyone in the story dies. But tonight was the happy ending night where they found a new place to live and would only let people in the new place that respected the forest and their way of life. I wish there really were places like that.

I never knew the real ending of the book until I was way older.

Dinker asked, "Do you think that Dr. Seuss minds that we make up the ending every time? I mean, he shouldn't, since we are missing pages and all."

"He seems like a cool guy. I don't think he'd mind."

"I hope he is a cool guy."

"He is."

I sounded so sure.

Dinker gave me a kiss on the cheek and went to bed. Before I left her room I asked her about Father O'Touches-a-lot. She said not to worry.

I should've.

I snuck out of her room, and as soon as the door was closed, Sister Satan grabbed me by the ear with ninja-like stealth and brought me into a room to beat on me. She loved whooping on my butt. S.S. ranted and raved on how I shouldn't touch Dinker.

Sister Satan was a funny one. She would beat me and Peewee for seeing each other's wieners, and then just me when I hugged Dinker, but she always turned a blind eye to  Father O'Touches-a-lot.

CHAPTER 9
Lucky's Halloween Special

Halloween is a little different for orphans, or "the poor," than it is for any normal wage-earning family, simply in that it's not fun, it's work. The costumes were planned a year in advance. No one had enough money to actually buy anything, you just had to salvage—which is a nice way of saying steal—stuff that looked useful. You traded with others to get what you needed, and just hoped that no one would steal your stuff for your costume before the last day of October. Most kids would end up having to shred one of their own shirts for a cloth mask or something—that is, only if someone else hadn't already stolen the shirt you were planning to shred!

Tips: as mentioned before with masks, ideally anything that covers your face is the best. Plan the route out by hitting up the rich houses first. The less memorable your Halloween costume, the better; then you can count on them not remembering you when you hit up the same house again a second time. Though, ideally, you may just want to have multiple costumes. Also plan out your safe drops because your bags can get crazy heavy and will most likely leave you an easy target for grab-bagging. Songs to raise morale are recommended. We used to chant "Candy, candy, candy," like Garfield from *Garfield's Halloween Adventure.*

My costumes were mostly handmade and consisted of Spider-Man, Super Mario, Link from *The Legend of Zelda,* a pointy-hooded ghost, U.S. Marine, and Mike Tyson.

Mike Tyson was the only legit store-bought mask, and when I say "legit store-bought mask" what that really means is that I stole it from a yard sale. Years later, when Tyson was accused of a crime, I went to school in a prisoner's uniform, boxing gloves, and his prison number, which was just the password to fight Tyson from *Punch-Out!!* : 007 373 5963. Most people found it funny, until I took off the mask and they saw I was white. Then they said I was racist. I was sent to the principal's office.

I sat in front of the school principal and my teacher as they argued for twenty minutes as to whether, and how, I should be disciplined. I was forced to take off the mask and hand in the uniform. I wasn't wearing anything underneath, so I had to wear the extra clothes they had at the school, which was really just my pick of stuff from last year's lost and found box. In today's society, I would have been expelled and it might have made national news. Poor kids today. Or maybe it was poor me back then. I could have been on TV!

On a normal Halloween, we would have brought as many eggs and as much toilet paper as we could carry, so when someone complained that it was too early or too late to be trick-or-treating, we would egg their house and car and TP their tree and phone lines. But in that infamous year of the Nintendo, we (I) wanted to impress Santa with our goodness and so we didn't stockpile any ammo.

Does Santa really watch all the kids when they're sleeping? He must be one creepy son of a gun.

That year though, me, Peewee, and Dinker hit the jackpot and found the ultimate Halloween treasure. Dinker found one house in the neighborhood with a bowl of candy sitting on the porch with a sign reading Please Take Only One. In our neighborhood, this was a horrible idea, because the first kids who got there always took all of the candy and everyone who followed got upset and ended up egging and TP-ing the house.

Peewee was ecstatic when he saw the bowl. He grabbed it with a huge smile and would have dumped it in his bag if I hadn't knocked his arm. The bowl tipped and some candy spilled out onto the floor. Peewee looked at me all confused.

"We can only take one," I said.

"What the hell?" Peewee asked.

"Yeah bro, what the hell is right," Dinker said to me.

"Only one each, Peewee, or we're not getting that Nintendo."

"What?"

"Oh, that's right. Santa," Dinker said.

Peewee looked disappointed, but nodded his head. He picked up what candy was spilled and put the bowl back. Then he grabbed for one piece of candy. Me and Dinker grabbed one for ourselves before doing an about-face and walking off the porch like a good little boy and girl. We left knowing we lost a true Halloween treasure. Some kids not far behind ran past us as we walked off that porch. They took all of the candy and called us morons.

Peewee was pissed.

"A lot of good Santa did us. Now those kids got all the candy!"

"Yeah, that's bullcrap," Dinker said, shaking her Jersey fist at them. I have no idea where she learned it.

I didn't have the guts to say anything, because Peewee and Dinker were right.

Those other kids ran by us and mocked us again. I didn't hesitate to say to Peewee and Dinker, "Get 'em!"

We chased those four other kids down, gave them a minor beating, took all their candy, and let them run away.

It was over very quickly. Dinker and Peewee laughed and gave high fives. Dinker looked into the bags of our newly plundered booty and spoke up.

"Should we take the candy back?"

I thought for a few seconds. I could tell by their expressions that they were hoping to keep the candy.

"Well . . . we took the candy from thieves and not from the nice people, so I think Santa will understand."

Peewee and Dinker smiled with relief. I think our group morale shot through the roof right then.

In my high spirits, later witnessing Korean Jen holding hands and kissing some guy named Chris was worse than a sucker punch to the gut. I was jealous. Dinker asked if I was okay. I said yes, but the truth is, I wasn't okay. Later I made out with Italian Jen to try and make Korean Jen jealous, but also because Italian Jen was wowzer crazy good looking. I was never a ladies' man growing up, but always got a girl on Halloween.

The guy, Chris, who moved in on my Korean Jen, was a great guy and everyone loved him. Everyone. Really. Guys and girls. Honestly, the kindest, coolest guy you could meet. So I am not proud of the fact that a week later, when I realized my plan to make Korean Jen jealous that Halloween had failed, I asked Chris, "Head or gut?"

Now, if you've been paying attention, "Head or gut?" was Jersey code for "I am going to hit you for doing me wrong. Please allow me to honor you by giving you the option of choosing your preferred body area for infliction of pain." Head-or-gut was the law of the land.

Chris knew exactly what this was about. I think he may have even seen this day coming. He said "gut," and I got him with a good one. It felt like my hand went up into his rib cage. He had to take a knee and couldn't breathe right for a few minutes. It felt great and horrible at the same time and afterwards we became good friends. That was the cool thing about head-or-gut, bygones were then bygones. I wish the head-or-gut deal was worldwide. Maybe we could end all wars. I read about them having duels with sabers and pistols a long time ago. I think they even did them in America—even some president did, I think. I cannot figure out for the life of me why they ever decided to do away with them.

## CHAPTER 10
### Christmas Day Part 2

Fast-forward. Christmas, early morning.

I was up all night thinking of the comebacks I could have used over the past week. I hated it when people always got the last word in. I needed to up my game with more "yo mama" jokes. Sadly, this is something I still do to this very day. I've always dreamed of having a time machine, but for all the wrong reasons. Some people dream of ruling the human race, or becoming crazy rich.

Maybe you wanna kill Hitler or save JFK in order to save several million lives. If I had a time machine, I would use it like a Reset button on the Nintendo to keep going back to the beginning till I had the perfect life. I could make sure I always had the wittier last word in those silly name-calling fights you have as kids—and that some people have even as adults.

I couldn't lie still in bed, so I went to creating my famed monster card game. It was a game where you started by collecting monsters in their baby forms, and then you'd battle others players who'd be trying to make their monsters stronger by battling them against each other. You could steal their monster under certain conditions, or your monster could eat theirs and make itself absorb the powers of the other monster. He would get stronger and look stronger by growing things like horns, extra tails, wings, and armor plating. I was generally secretive about it, which was only because I knew that if S.S. found out, she'd beat my butt red for devil worship or something.

I did show Biggie and Peewee once. I didn't have a name for the game at the time and they had so much fun playing the game they dubbed it Monster Masters. Dinker and Korean Jen thought it was the dumbest thing ever. I thought about finding a way to sell the monsters, but when I told Biggie about it, he told me no one would ever buy the game.

Many, many years later, when Biggie was still living close to me, he ran into my house screaming, "Lucky, you must be rich!" Those exact words. I was confused and asked him what he was talking about. He screamed that my game was huge and that everyone was buying it. I asked him more about it. That was the first time I ever heard the word "Pokémon."

"What *is* Pokéman?" I asked.

I found out it was one of the most popular games in the world from Japan, and it led to movies, video games, and every product imaginable. How about that Reset button time machine right about now?

I looked at the clock. It was around three in the morning. I tried to wake Peewee up, but he was a sleeping machine; with the exception of last year's Christmas, as soon as his head hit the pillow he was out and wouldn't wake up until the wake-up call.

I snuck out of the boys' room as quietly as I could. I passed by two nuns on watch that night and heard them gossiping about Sister Satan. It was enough dirt for blackmail and it brought joy to my heart. Were it any other night, I would've gladly stayed to listen to the whole thing, but I was on a mission to see Santa—or at least to be the first to see the Nintendo.

I peeked in on Dinker to see if she was up. She was a light sleeper like me, but she was all out, cuddling with Blacky. Blacky, who now had a Band-Aid over the pencil stab wound. Blacky, with a face all dented up. He looked as normal as a doll could after the beatings that Dinker occasionally administered.

I closed the door slowly, making sure not to wake her, then I ran down the stairs pretending to be a ninja. I was a running shadow and the only thing on my mind was that Nintendo.

I figured I must have just missed Santa, because no one was around, not even a mouse. I always wanted to say that.

I started sifting through the gifts, looking for anything Nintendo-shaped. When I couldn't find my present after a few minutes, I started to panic. I was wading in the mess of sour-smelling news-wrapping paper. I was making a mess, and a whole lot of noise as well.

I was about to throw in the towel when, in anger, I instead threw a gift that couldn't have been a Nintendo across the room.

What the hell? There must be some mistake. Was it too late to call the North Pole? I was so confused. I did *everything*. What more could that jolly bastard want?

I got so angry I started tearing at random presents in fury. Out from the first shredded wrapping paper: dress socks.

"Dress socks?! Dress socks?!"

I didn't care whether the nuns found me or not anymore. Let them see the rage. I never felt so betrayed in my life, and this is coming from a guy whose parents *abandoned him*!

I lost it. Anger turned into tears. Not sad tears, but the type of tears a man cries when he has nothing left to lose. The kind of tears people get when they hit the bottom and then the bottom falls out. I threw those crummy socks against the wall with as much force as anyone can throw a pair of socks.

I jumped into the Christmas tree in hopes of tearing it down. I smashed every thin glass ornament. I opened all the gifts, looking for my promised Nintendo. I knew it probably

wasn't going to be there, but I was desperate. I rampaged over top of everyone's presents. I ripped down every Christmas decoration and tore them with my bare hands. If I couldn't be happy on Christmas, no one else could be either.
In the middle of punching a used Teddy Ruxpin that didn't work, it hit me. Reality hit me.

Every punch I threw at that smelly used bear I started mumbling out loud to myself.

"The Nintendo. Peewee. Dinker. The others."

Every name was another punch. "Dennis."

Oh, crap, Dennis! He was going to kill me.

How in the hell no one ever heard me downstairs causing a ruckus is a mystery to me to this day.

I looked out the window and across the street. A plastic lit-up Santa was hanging in the window of a building's first floor. I stared into the eyes of that lifeless plastic Santa. His blue eyes weren't even painted in the lines where they should have been.

"Screw you, Santa, I'm doing this myself," I said. I had hatched a plan. I snuck outside.

It was a beautiful New Jersey winter night. There was a light dusting of snow on the ground, barely noticeable, but for the most part, it was a clear and slightly chilly night. Everyone was asleep, or at least it seemed like it. Even the no-good street thugs who loved to rob the tourists who drank too much were probably in their beds for a long winter's nap.

Really, everyone should walk around their city or neighborhood after hours, There is something romantic in the freedom and power you feel. Maybe that's why those no-good street thugs prefer it. It gives you time to reflect. I was doing a lot of that, since Santa had screwed me over only a few minutes before.

I took a breather at the same curb that Korean Jen kissed me at. I thought, would Dennis really kill me? What should I do? Run away? What about Dinker and Peewee? They needed me, right? What if Dennis just hurt me bad and I was fine in a few weeks? What if he hurt me bad and I wasn't? What if I wound up like Muscle Car? But, either way, my reputation for getting things done would be ruined. My reputation was gold so far. If I lost that, I'd lose it for good. I didn't even know if Peewee and Dinker could forgive me then.

Then it hit. It hit me like a Mike Tyson uppercut, which is another way of saying it blew my mind, knocked my socks off, and nearly popped my eyeballs out. It was an idea so horrible that it was awesome.

*I would steal a Nintendo.*

Korean Jen's family was always so easy to steal off of, and that was even *before* I had their trust! Even my justification was quick. I mean, after all, they had *three* Nintendos. Who needs *three* Nintendos? I was sure they'd understand, with my life being on the line and all. Not to mention that I had kissed Korean Jen, and that made me kind of part of the family. That's even before taking into account that we were sworn cousins anyway.

I ran to Korean Jen's house before I even wrapped up my thoughts. Truth be told, I would have stolen that Nintendo whether I could justify it to myself or not. It was true what that kid said: I was a rat bastard.

I picked the lock and snuck in. I know what you're asking yourself—how can someone as young as myself back then pick a lock? Let me tell you something about New Jersey; if you haven't stolen a car or broken into a house by the time you're eight, you may as well be in SPED classes. Of course this was ironic, because I had helped break into a house before I was seven, and I was still put in SPED classes.

I got some plastic shopping bags out of the kitchen and headed to the living room because the living room Nintendo would be the easiest one of the three to steal. I paused in awe.

That whole room was the most perfect Christmas

display anyone would have ever seen. It freaking looked like the North Pole! They had Santa, elves, reindeer, Mrs. Claus, baby Jesus with the Wise Men; they even had the Jewish candle thing—which I find to be very funny now. Korean Jen's mom's collection of carousels was even spinning. It was a happy holiday heaven. Even a department store couldn't have put something together that good, especially in New Jersey.

And what was even more perfect, was that the tree was so big and bright it made the room super easy to see. I went straight for the Nintendo. I started unhooking everything and putting it in the plastic bags. Then I heard someone coming. I panicked and didn't know where to hide. I remembered reading that if you stay still no one will see you, so I ducked behind a floor lamp and didn't move.

Crap. It was Korean Jen's mom. Damn, and she was wearing next to nothing. Red satin undies and a bra. That was it!

She went to the sink for some water. To this day, I have never seen such a hot woman.

That image of her got me through many lonely nights. In the summer, I used to camp out in front of her house hoping to catch a peek of her, and the stuff I did in that tent while thinking of her was stuff that would have got me sent straight to hell if Sister Satan ever found out. I swear, with S.S. every damn loophole was filled. You couldn't be with other boys. You couldn't be with other girls. You couldn't even be all by yourself.

Korean Jen's dad was my role model because he was nerdy like me and not the best looking man, but somehow got a woman like that to fall in love with him. Whenever I asked girls out, and no matter how many times they'd say no, it didn't get me down too much, because if someone like Korean Jen's dad could get someone like Korean Jen's mom, then I stood a chance at getting someone hot too.

Seeing Korean Jen's mom on Christmas Eve was a

present enough. Korean Jen's mom was sexy, beautiful, and by that time had also seen me. Not only did she see me, she saw my excited friend in my sweat pants.

She almost dropped her glass.

"Lucky, what the hell are you doing?"

God, if this scene could have only played out like in those VHS tapes Biggie hid under his bed the year after.

I was embarrassed, and had nowhere to run. I came clean and told Korean Jen's mom everything, the whole time staring at her goods. She never covered herself, and after I had finished the story, she laughed. Korean Jen's dad overheard the laughter and came downstairs. He was wearing tight green man undies and had some crazy hair growth on the inside of his thighs. It was hard to look without cringing. Unfortunately, he seemed to care as little about what he was wearing as she did. After Korean Jen's dad heard the story, he laughed. Korean Jen's parents were so cool.

Korean Jen's dad kissed Korean Jen's mom on the cheek, then bit her on the neck like he was a vampire.

"See you in bed," he said.

And that rear view of him walking up the stairs was even worse than the front view.

I had no idea what was going on between them at that time, but now I can appreciate just how lucky of a bastard Korean Jen's dad was. He was getting ready to get it on.

Korean Jen's mom put her arm around me.

"Lucky, I'm going to let you take the Nintendo and five games on *one* condition."

"Anything! You want your car washed? You want me to shovel your driveway when it snows? You want me to cut your grass?"

I would have given up my firstborn to her for a Nintendo and her hotness.

"You can never date Jen, Lucky. She deserves a better boyfriend than you."

I was in shock. The request hurt me. The truth always does. I started calming down a bit. "Do you understand?" she asked me.

I squeaked, "Yes."

She kneeled and started packing up the Nintendo for me. I was in a trance staring at her sexiness.

"Get your games," she said.

I tried to concentrate. These would probably be the only five games I'd ever have unless somebody stole more. Up to this point, it was the biggest decision of my life, and all I could think of was sneaking another peek at Korean Jen's mom.

I looked into their game drawer—yes, they even had the official Nintendo game drawer. "You have five gold copies of *The Legend of Zelda*. Who the hell needs five of the same game?"

Korean Jen's mom was starting to get a bit annoyed. Either my cuteness had worn off or she really had something to do in bed—which she did.

"Just pick five and leave," she said coldly.

I hit a home run by picking the best five video games ever made, in my honest opinion: *Super Mario Bros., Excitebike, Ice Hockey, The Legend of Zelda*, and *Mike Tyson's Punch-Out!!*

I snuck one more good peek at Korean Jen's mom's goods before heading back to the orphanage to get my hero's welcome. Yessir, I would be a set man for life there.

## CHAPTER 11
### Lucky the Christmas Miracle

I didn't make it back in time to see this next part I'm about to tell you, but Peewee and Dinker later told me everything. Apparently back at the orphanage, there was complete panic. The place was a mess and Christmas was ruined for everyone. Some of the younger children were in tears looking at their torn-open presents and broken toys from Santa. The nuns were running around clueless, just hoping they wouldn't lose control of the older kids. Many of the nuns used to say that if you don't get adopted by the time you are ten, you are on a path to pure evil; I was over ten. Christmas that day was the nuns' testament to my evil. I may as well have been that Damien kid from the *Omen* film.

From outside I could hear Sister Satan screaming, "Where is Lucky?" And at that very moment, I kicked the door in and held the Nintendo up over my head like Link from *The Legend of Zelda* would do with a treasure he just found—or like the New Jersey Devils would do with a Stanley Cup when they won. An imaginary 'Hallelujah Chorus' was playing in the background and everything.

Seeing what was in my hands someone shouted, "It's a Christmas miracle!"

The other orphans surrounded me, cheering my name and carrying me around like a hero. Peewee shouted, "That's my brother!"

They put me on that stupid stage I had sat down with Santa on. I held the Nintendo above my head again to work the crowd. I could see Sister Satan in the back gathering all the nuns together. She didn't look too happy. Peewee climbed the stage and really got them going by saying, "My brother did it! He got Santa to get us a Nintendo!"

I shouted, "Fudge Santa!"—but I used another word and it wasn't "fudge." Everyone was in shock over what I said and having said it so loud. I tried to fill in the awkward silence. "*I* did it! That fat bastard just got me socks!"

The children start chanting "SAN-TA SUCKS!"

Sister Satan stormed up and grabbed me by the ear to pull me off the stage. She was gonna make me wash my mouth with soap. But then something happened. The other kids, following Dennis's lead, blocked her. S.S. had a lot of power, but even she knew she was outnumbered. This was not the moment to test us. We were united. Powerful people who abuse their power always are afraid of the weak being united, because it exposes them for who they truly are, phony cowards.

S.S. let go of my ear and tried to calm the hostile crowd. "Don't forget the real reason for the season."

Dennis didn't need to step forward. He was already leading the mob of a bunch of parentless kids. "You lied to us about Santa! How do we know you didn't lie to us about Jesus too?" I could tell he'd wanted to ask S.S. that question for a while.

S.S. knew she'd lost control. We orphans took over the orphanage that day. The nuns backed down for now because they knew an orphanage is like a prison, except it doesn't have bars, and they were the guards with no guns—although they did have rulers. We all could kinda guess the nuns would have their revenge on all of us someday, but that moment, that was our time of glory.

S.S. paced back and forth, she couldn't let it go. Most

of the nuns just let the situation roll off them, but not S.S. She never let it go. She went out in the cold like an old angry penguin, looking for a payphone. She was calling the police.

In the meantime, we were busy hooking up the Nintendo. It took forever. We had no instructions and none of us had ever hooked up any video game system before. Only a few of us had actually even seen the back of the television. It's so obvious now, but to us kids back then, it was like a Rubik's Cube in the dark. We were swearing up a storm and were about ready to kick that damn ancient television over when I put a wire in the right spot. The screen flickered and everyone cheered. We could see *Excitebike* on the screen. We were so excited—no pun intended—that a very obvious question wasn't asked until at least minutes later.

"Where's the sound?" Dennis asked. He and I had first dibs with the game.

Of course, Bucky was there, and had the glory of plugging things in correctly. The speakers crackled at first, then the most beautiful music filled our ears. It was to become the music of our childhood.

Then the cops came.

There is one thing the poor learn before the rich, and that is to hate cops. When us orphans saw the "pigs and bacon" come into the orphanage, we were understandably upset. It's especially worse now. If it were cops now, they would have just pepper sprayed and beaten us, but back then, there was some honor in being a police officer and *actually working with the community*. They came offering us gifts to calm us down. Interesting enough, none of the gifts was a Nintendo.

Everyone's always told not to take candy from a stranger, and to never give the cops anything—especially information, but no one ever said anything about taking things from cops. To our surprise, the cops started throwing us stocking stuffers. They were cheap dollar store toys but we still loved them, especially the cap guns and army men!

Sister Satan was so angry and snappy with the police. "You're not here to be Santa! You're here to lock up this criminal!" she said, pointing at me.

S.S. and the two cops took me into another room away from everyone. Dennis whispered in my ear as I was being led away.

"Scream, if you need us."

I'm sure the cops and S.S. overheard him. I have no idea what he would have or could have done anyway, but his confidence was impressive. I mentioned that Dennis and I had first dibs, but it was really Dennis alone who had first dibs now because I was being interrogated by the police.

We were in the other room: Sister Satan, two cops, and poor old me. The white cop, who looked pretty reserved seconds ago, flipped the switch from loving and caring cop to angry white cop. Him and Sister Satan just started screaming at me. The other cop, who was a black cop, was trying to calm the situation down. I hid behind him as Sister Satan and White Cop were accusing me of—and this was the first time I ever heard the word—larceny.

I went over to the black cop because he was the only one who didn't look like he was gonna bite my head off.

I peeked my head from around the black cop and shouted, "What about the Tenth Amendment?"

This stupid statement shut S.S. and White Cop up for a second or two. I thought I had them where I wanted them. Black Cop looked at me and recited the Tenth like he was taking a civics test: "The powers not delegated to the United States by the Constitution, nor prohibited by it to the States, are reserved to the States respectively, or to the people."

I shouted victoriously, "Yeah!" It was like I just defeated the justice system, but when I looked up at the black cop he was shaking his head.

Sister Satan was clenching her rosary. "Oh, thank you

baby Jesus. I can finally rid myself of this hell-demon of a child."

White Cop spoke. "Listen up, whatever your name is. We're going to lock you up and throw away the key."

And then he barked. I wish I was making that part up, but he barked at me. Like a dog.

Lucky for me, Black Cop was the diplomat. "Bill, just let me ask the questions so we can end this and get back to Wawa." So White Cop's name was Bill.

Sister Satan and White Cop both grunted, then S.S. started pacing the room. Looking back, those two could have seriously hit it off and gotten married.

The black cop took a knee, looked me in the eyes, and lowered his voice. "Where did you get the Nintendo?"

I thought really hard about my answer, but I didn't really need to.

"I got it from Santa," I said.

I tried to look to S.S. without her noticing. I wanted to try and check her mood. Not surprisingly, she looked furious.

"Tell me the truth, kid. I can't help you if you don't tell me the truth."

I am so embarrassed of what I did next. I have never told another soul of the horrendous thing I did next, because if any of the others knew, they would have killed me. I told the truth.

"He lies!" Sister Satan's voice was sounding squawky.

So much for "the truth shall set you free." The black cop held up his hand to S.S. to shut her up. He stood up and straightened his pants. "We will look into it," he said and turned for the door.

White Cop spoke. "If you are lying . . . oh boy, oh boy!"

I know that White Cop didn't have anything to say anymore because that is what everyone does when they don't have any good comebacks.

Black Cop and White Cop left the orphanage, I guess to go to Korean Jen's house. I got out of the room as soon as I could and went for the Nintendo, but Sister Satan grabbed my ear, twisted it, and led me to an empty chair. I sat waiting for exactly fifty-one minutes and sixteen seconds.

I know this, because as long as there's a clock where I can see it, I always stare at the time when I get nervous.

The black cop returned. A big smile was on his face. White Cop was nowhere to be seen. Two good signs.

"Thank you for waiting, Sister. The family is insisting that the Nintendo is a gift to the boy."

This put Sister Satan in an even more rotten mood.

"That woman dresses like a whore," she said.

"I'm sorry, ma'am, there's nothing to be done. It's an odd story I'll admit, but it's Christmas.

The family is not pressing charges."

S.S. lost it, that poor bag. She started screaming, "What about the decorations and presents he destroyed?"

"Can you prove that he did it? And if he did, that seems to be more of a family in-house type of issue."

"So you're worthless! What a waste of time and taxpayers' money!"

The black cop eyed me with approval. "Well, you have a good day, ma'am," he said.

Then he left the orphanage.

I felt good. I felt real good. I didn't say it out loud, but I certainly thought it: I was untouchable.

Sister Satan flashed a twisted smile.

"God gives everyone what they deserve, Lucky!"

I tried to take what she said in a positive light, but it was hard to, because coming from S.S., it sounded more like a curse.

And what would you know? I was right.

S.S. came charging at me, screaming. The other nuns

ran in to try to stop her from kicking me, but S.S. was on a rampage and unstoppable. I was on the floor getting jabbed in the ribcage with her hard-ass shoes.

As I looked up at those nuns while they watched me in pain getting kicked around by Sister Satan, that was the first time in my life I realized that not all cops and religious people are evil. It's just that the good ones are always frightened or bullied into doing evil things.

# CHAPTER 12
## Meeting Brett

After the holidays, I was back to my old self. Wait, scratch that. After the holidays, I was worse than ever. It was a new year, but trying to be good got me nowhere. I realized after Christmas that if I ever wanted anything in life from that point on, I'd have to take it or fight for it. I was proud to be the ultimate street rat. I stole whatever I wanted. I fought those weaker than me to take what they had. To say I was skipping school is an understatement. I was more like leaping over the semesters.

I was a monster. I think all that pent-up badness from that whole year of being good for the Nintendo finally exploded inside me. Worst of all, my daydreaming about my chances with Korean Jen were officially over. With all that said, part of my daily mission in life was to pass on some misery to Sister Satan. I broke into and messed up her bedroom, stole her underwear and hung it outside for the whole neighborhood to see, and whenever she hung up laundry into the mud it went.

Honestly, anything I could do to ruin her life, I did. I think I pushed her to the limit. She couldn't get any angrier with me than she already was. The best part is, I was practically immune to her now. And because S.S. was always miserable and being a terrible "Bride of Christ," the other nuns now started shunning her. Sister Satan's influence in the orphanage was growing weak.

One day S.S. called me into her office. I knew immediately it was gonna be bad news, but I didn't expect what came next. A man with curly blond hair, green eyes, and a poofy mustache sat in one of the office chairs. His clothes were ragged and stained. He smelled only slightly better than Santa did when I asked for my Nintendo.

Who in the hell was this guy? My imagination was running wild. As it did, I started growing more and more scared with what was going on. I hoped to hell that this man wasn't here to adopt me. Even worse, maybe S.S. paid this guy to act like he was adopting me but he was actually gonna tie me to a cinder block and have me "sleep with the fishies," as they say.

"Are you here to kill me?"

His eyes opened wide and his mustache twitched as he opened his mouth. His teeth were dark brown in the cracks between his teeth.

He didn't answer me, so I tried with another question.

"Am I gonna get beat?"

The man looked confused and turned to Sister Satan. S.S. smiled liked the devil and let out a fake laugh and shook her head.

"He has such an active imagination," she said to the man.

The man spoke up, his voice is kinda hard to describe. It was really deep, but sounded meek at the same time.

"You beat them?" he asked.

S.S. let out another nervous/fake laugh. I noticed she only laughed when she was trying to cover something up. She gave me a quick death stare and uttered a solid, "No."

I rolled my eyes and opened my big mouth. I wasn't afraid of S.S. anymore, and just having heard that guy talk, he didn't have the balls to do diddly-squat to me.

"She beats me like every day, dude. She hates her life

and beats all us for it."

The man had little interest in what I had to say and turned back to Sister Satan.

"Lucky, this man, Brett, is thinking of adopting you," S.S. said.

Okay, my initial fear was completely justified.

"Why me? Hey, mister. There are so many better kids than me to choose from. Is she trying to pawn me off on you?" I turned to Sister Satan. "I'm over ten years old! I thought you said I wouldn't get adopted and was on a path to evil?"

"Lucky, everyone deserves to find a family."

I tried to think of a way to say that I didn't wanna go with this Brett guy in a way that wouldn't piss him off.

"Mister, I don't know you, but you can get a better make and model than me. This woman is trying to sell you a lemon!"

S.S. took a big step towards me. "Lucky!"

"What? Like this is the best you could find? Why do I have to go with *this* guy?" "Lucky, I'm your father."

Reality check.

I hulked out. I was so angry that I started punching myself in the face. I saw a glass bowl of M&M'S on the desk. I reached for it and shattered it over my forehead. Candy and glass went everywhere. Blood trickled down from my head. The hate poured into me quicker than I could process. I was going berserk. I screamed at him. Blood and spit flew outta my mouth.

"This isn't how we should meet! I should be famous and rich! You ruined everything, you dirty dick!"

I'd never called anyone a dirty dick before. I had thought of it a month ago and was planning on using it the next time I had to trash-talk someone.

I ran out of the room. Outside there were nuns on standby. They grabbed me and held me to keep me from hurting myself any more. It's funny; aside from Sister Satan, I never bothered remembering the other nuns' names, but I will always remember how they held me and how much I needed it. They, the nuns, patched me up, and once I calmed down Sister Satan brought me back in.

Brett was still there, and looked more disturbed than before, if I do say so myself. I guess S.S. wasn't done selling this cow for those magic beans. She hated me so much she probably would have given me up to a monkey on meth. The three of us sat in the room. It was real quiet. Brett looked like a dried-up piece of crap. He didn't try to play it off like he wasn't one either. I could appreciate his honesty at least. Not like S.S., who looked like a dried piece of crap but tried to act like she wasn't.

Ultimately, it was me who finally broke the silence by turning to Brett. "Where the hell have you been?"

Brett twiddled his thumbs. I guess he was asking himself if he should lie or tell the truth. "Rehab," he said.

I was surprised by his honesty, but his answer only proved what I already knew: this guy was lower than scum.

"You've been in rehab my whole life?"

I don't know if Brett couldn't make eye contact or just didn't want to. "Your mother left me with you, and—"

"Why?"

"I had a temper and beat her up a bit . . ."

There was a look he gave me. It was a look of a man who was defeated and had nothing left of value. What a pitiful man. He continued.

"I hit rock bottom and couldn't take care of you anymore."

He began to cry and I just thought to myself, I came from this weak person? I hope no one finds out. Hell, who was I kidding? News of me going schizo was probably all over the orphanage. They'd have everything figured out by now.

Brett went on.

"I'm trying, I really am . . . I'm trying my best to make

everything right."

Somebody give this man a tissue! You're embarrassing yourself! I wanted so bad to say those things, but I held back.

We sat in pure silence for three minutes and fifty-six seconds. I looked at Sister Satan. She was nodding her head in approval. Approval of what?

I asked Brett, "How did I wind up here?"

He wiped away some tears. He was still refusing to look me in the eye.

"I left you in one of the casino hotels, hoping they would know what to do with you. A few days later I read they found you. You were nearly dead."

He began crying again. I don't know what I hated more, his weakness or being such a scumbag to leave his own flesh and blood in a random casino hotel. Hearing this also made me feel more worthless than I normally felt as an orphan. I almost didn't care what he had to say anymore. I didn't really wanna know any more. But he kept talking.

"I told myself that someone would adopt you and take better care of you since you were on the news and all."

"Well, you thought wrong."

He wept even harder. What a baby.

"I know," he said.

"You're very weak," I said.

I needed to hurt Brett's feelings in any way I could. "Lucky!" S.S. yelled.

"All I'm saying is, why tell me all this?"

Brett's face was red. "One of the twelve steps is telling others sorry about how you wronged them or something like that."

"So you think you can be a dad now?" I asked.

"I've been sober for a few months now. I have two jobs and I know I'm on the right path."

Sister Satan cut in, "No one is getting adopted today. It is just one day with your father." I had to correct her. "No, it's one day with a man named Brett."

She smiled at me. I always wondered what she was thinking when she smiled. "It is one day with Brett." She paused and then went on. "Lucky, everyone deserves to be adopted, even you."

Gee, thanks.

"You just want to get rid of me," I said.

"But, of course," S.S. said, opening the door. I guess that was our cue.

I mocked her smile and then stood up to leave the room with Brett.

As we walked out, I was so embarrassed because I took so much pride in being an orphan. I felt like I sold out on my own kind. The worst part is, I was right about everyone knowing what was going on. They all guessed he was my real father already because of how bad he looked. Only two kinds of people walk out of an orphanage with a kid: ones who look like they have their life together, and people whose lives are falling apart at the seams. It doesn't take a genius to figure out which group Brett fell under.

Dinker and Peewee were by the exit, waiting with a look of suspicion. As I walked behind Brett, Dinker punched me real hard in the head to remind me of our pact. Peewee just said, "Remember the pact!" I don't know if Brett didn't see Dinker clock me, or *chose* not to see it. People in our neighborhood saw a lot of things, but always chose not to see most of it. Whatever helps you sleep at night, I guess.

I gave a guarantee to Peewee and Dinker that I would always be me and keep my word. In others words, the pact was safe. As I was leaving with Brett, I overheard Sister Satan tell Dinker and Peewee, "Say goodbye to your so-called brother. He won't be coming back." But I knew it was a lie.

We walked to Brett's car, if you could call it that. It was mostly rust with some gray primer. I was embarrassed and he could tell by my loud sighs.

Nothing eases the pain of existence like a good joke. If Brett hadn't told me his joke, I probably would've turned back to the orphanage right there.

"So tell me, Brett Jr., are you a FORD man or a Chevy man?"

Brett calling me Brett Jr. really chapped my hide. I had to lay down some rules.

"My name is Lucky. I don't care what a birth certificate says and I sure as hell don't care what you or my mother named me. Do you understand?"

That proud look disappeared. He was shaken up, but still wanted to lighten the mood. "Okay, okay. So Lucky, are you a FORD man or a Chevy man?"

"Well, BRETT! I have never really thought about it! What do you say?!" I yelled. I was being so damn obnoxious.

"I have this here FORD, but at heart, I am a bona fide Chevy man! One day I hope to have a really nice Corvette. If I got a 'Vette I could turn everything around."

I never knew or found out the difference between FORD and Chevy, but if anyone asked after that day, I was a FORD guy solely out of spite for Brett.

He opened the back door to his piece of crap. Back door?

"I can't sit up front?"

"Sorry, little pal. I have a fish tank I picked up and it needs to stay up front because it can't hold on like you."

That was weird of him to say, but I didn't ask any questions. I hopped in. Much to my freakin' astonishment, there was a huge rusted hole in the floor. It looked like someone had spilled acid in there.

"Hey, what gives?"

Brett laughed. It was a redneck laugh, if I ever heard one. Like a yuck-yuck-yuck type of laugh topped off with a snort.

"It's a Flintstone car!" he said.

For some reason, his life sucking was hilarious to him.

We got in the car and closed the doors. Brett looked back to me.

"Hold on tight, pal!" he yelled, like he was one of those people doing the rides at Six Flags, with the serious face. Like if I didn't seriously behave myself I could get seriously hurt. "You drop anything down there and it's gone for good. And of course I wouldn't want to lose you!"

Yeah, sure . . . like that time at the hotel casino?

I clicked the loose seat belt, tried to grip the cushion with my small hands, and pressed my feet behind the driver's seat. That was about as secure as I was gonna be.

"'Atta boy!" Brett said.

I couldn't stand the way he talked.

I thought I'd never hate anyone more than Sister Satan, but Brett was so stupid I almost started missing her. The damn seat belt wouldn't even adjust properly. I held on for dear life as we pulled away.

As we got more and more into unfamiliar neighborhoods Brett's conversations got more and more boring. I couldn't stop staring at that hole of death beneath me. Manholes in the street were just dark blurs looking through the floor. Brett went on about his fish tank. He had some horrible business idea of stealing people's trash, fixing it up, and then selling it back to them because he knew they didn't have it anymore.

Goddammit, that hole was terrifying!

The fish tank that occupied the front seat was filthy, with a thick coat of green on it. It was filled up with old coffee cups, parking tickets, and whatever trash he was too lazy to throw down the hole, I guess. This is a joke, but he probably had a court summons stashed in there, what with all the parking tickets he had.

I started thinking about what would happen if Brett hit a pothole and I fell down the hole. He was going between thirty and forty. Would it instantly kill me? How painful would it be? Maybe less painful than listening to this hillbilly talk about his horrible business plans. The more I knew about him, the less I liked.

We made a quick stop at the 7-Eleven. I was glad to get out of that death trap alive or at least make it to a checkpoint.

"You ever been to a 7-Eleven?" Brett asked. Was he serious?

"I'm more of a Wawa guy," I said.

"No way, 7-Eleven is the best!"

Jesus, why the hell was he so enthusiastic?

As soon as we walked inside the 7-Eleven, I went down a separate aisle and pocketed three Snickers bars for me, Peewee, and Dinker. I peeked over to the counter and saw Brett and the cashier dude yukking it up, so I also decided to pocket a few packs of baseball and Garbage Pail Kids cards. I also pocketed the latest issue of *The Amazing Spider-Man*.

I went to Brett's side, hoping no one would be the wiser for my sticky fingers. Brett had a stupid smile on his face and patted my head like I were a dog or something. The cashier looked down at me with a warm smile.

"And you must be Brett Jr.! Who your proud daddy has been talking about so much. He wouldn't shut up about you."

Brett was blushing and had on a giant stupid smile. I could see all the brown divots between his teeth.

"Let's call him little B.J.," the cashier said. I hated that guy already.

"The name is Lucky," I said, showing a little attitude to hopefully stop them from giving me any more stupid names. B.J., wasn't that the one girl's name from *Full House*?

The attitude seemed to have worked, because Brett looked sad again. "Pete, this is Lucky," he said.

"What about Brett Jr.?"

"He likes to be called Lucky now."

"Oh . . ."

Insert awkward silence.

Brett let out a long sigh, probably thinking that maybe this "derelict father and orphan son bonding day" was a bad idea, but then quicker than you could bat an eye, he just bounced back to his stupid old self.

"Let's get Lucky some Reesie's Pee-cees and that bow and arrow set."

I hated it when people said "Reesie's Pee-cees," and not "Reese's Pieces"—like you're supposed to say it!

I remember looking to the cashier next, only because I couldn't think of a better place to look. The guy's name tag said Peter, which made sense.

Pete cleared his throat, but tried to talk quietly. You could tell he was a chain smoker. I was a regular Sherlock Holmes when it came to recognizing a person's vices.

"Brett, I can get you the candy, but your food stamps don't cover toys." Brett's voice became quiet too.

"Pete, help me out here. Just look the other way on this one."

"I'm already looking the other way with Lucky's pockets being filled with stuff from my store."

I just pretended to be clueless as to what he was talking about. You'd be amazed at what kinds of situations a good poker face can get you through. Too bad Jesus never said anything about a poker face being one of the great virtues, but maybe that's because that's what his secret was!

Brett pathetically nodded his head, agreeing.

"Okay, okay, okay. Just the candy then and could you please get me some matches too?"

When Pete turned to get the matches Brett moved quickly and put the bow and arrow set in the bags before anyone would notice. The bags barely rustled.

Ballsy move. Very smooth too. Maybe Brett wasn't

that bad of a guy.

We got back in his "deathtrap-mobile." Brett gave me the Reese's Pieces and my new toy. To this day, when I eat Reese's Pieces I think of Brett—not knowing how to properly say Reese's Pieces—and hope I am doing better than him.

The bow and arrow set came with an Indian headdress, a plastic bow, and five suction cup arrows. I opened it up inside the car and immediately lost one of the arrows down the Flintstone hole.

We finally made it to Brett's place. The house was huge. A bit old, but a surprisingly nice big country three-story house. For the second time since meeting him, I was impressed—the first time being when he stole the bow and arrow set for me. I really didn't expect this.

Across the street from the house was a fork in the road, and in the middle of it was a copper statue of some Native American chief. It was old and the same green as the Statue of Liberty. Brett noticed me staring at it. He put one hand on my shoulder. It bothered me that it was there, but I didn't say anything.

Brett told me the Indian's name was Chief Half-Ass. He told me he was the leader of the Manahawkin Tribe, and that the white man surrounded him near a lake. The white man gave the tribe the option to surrender to work for the white man, or to fight and die.

I don't know why, but I was so interested by the story, I blurted out,

"What happened next?"

Brett smiled and went on. He said that Chief Half-Ass screamed to the white men, "Today is a good day to die!"

The Manahawkin Indians fought to their deaths. Every one of them fought while their longhouse was burned down with their families inside.

I really doubt now that any of that is true, but I have heard that story many times from people in New Jersey since.

So who knows? Maybe it is true. Or maybe it's just some tall tale that was retold over and over again like the Jersey Devil, but I was so moved by that story.

"I hope one day I can be brave like those Manahawkin warriors," I said.

Brett patted me on the head and said, "I know you will be a warrior."

What a weird thing to say to your estranged kid.

We headed inside.

Once inside, everything came crashing back down to normal. The interior of the house was a wreck. It looked like it hadn't been cleaned in years. There was stuff everywhere and weird people who smelled bad with their sleeping bags everywhere. Brett took me into a tiny room. I mean, it was tiny! It was smaller than Dinker's! Brett's room didn't even have a window because his room was a freakin' closet.

"This is my place," he said with a smile.

He had a sleeping bag, dirty blankets, and a pillow all bunched up on one end of the floor. He had a Rebel flag—even though he was from New Jersey—hanging on his wall next to a poster of a giant Corvette. Those two things alone took up the whole wall. On the other end of the closet, there was a shelf with another dirty fish tank and some type of army helmet sitting next to it.

"Were you in the Army?" I asked.

He stuck out his chest, made direct eye contact with me, and said, "I am a Marine." It was only slightly impressive.

"Don't you mean 'was' a Marine?"

He snapped back, "Once a Marine, always a Marine."

I always imagined a Marine as some buff dude waking up at three a.m. every day, running eighteen miles in the rain, and putting his life on the line to protect others. Brett didn't even do a good job of protecting me. Not just "not a good job," he failed miserably!

"If you stay the night, you can sleep in the same sleeping bag I slept in when I was in the USMC."

"Maybe," I said, not even sure if I wanted to sleep here or not. S.S. said a day. Did she really mean it when she said I wasn't going back to the orphanage? Jeez, I didn't even want to know what the bathroom at Brett's place looked like. If I had to go in the middle of the night I was gonna do it out of a window.

I tried to keep the conversation going since Brett being a Marine was the only interesting thing about him so far. Maybe he could show me some special fighting moves, like that neck chop that makes people drop instantly.

"Were you a war hero?"

"Depends on who you ask."

Brett put his arm around me, hitting his knuckles off the wall of his narrow closet-bedroom and led me downstairs. I guess that was his way of saying *no*?

We watched *Transformers*, followed by *G.I. Joe* back to back. I had seen them both hundreds of times. At the end of *Transformers*, Megatron blew up an oil rig, sending the Autobots swimming. It was weird watching with Brett, because that episode had a father and son working the rig and the son tried to save his father when they were under attack by the Decepticons.

It was awkward because I think me and Brett both knew I probably wouldn't do something like that for him.

The *G.I. Joe* episode wasn't my favorite. Cobra Commander was threatening to steal monuments with his satellite. Brett said that Baroness was "one fine mamma" even though she was a bad guy.

It was the best hour I'd spent with Brett so far. For two cartoons I felt like I had a real father.

When the shows first started we had the room to ourselves, but by the time Joe ended with ". . . and knowing is half the battle," the place was packed with losers who smelled funny.

Everyone called me Brett Jr. or B.J., and for the only time in my life, I didn't correct them. Everyone was just happy to see me and they were especially proud of Brett. Brett felt good about doing the "right thing," as he repeated over and over to everyone. His face showed it too.

Someone turned on the stereo and started playing the Grateful Dead. Up to that point, I never heard music played as loud as they played it then. It was like the sound was gonna tear through the walls.

Some blonde lady that went by the name of Sunshine kept being grabby with Brett. She was average-looking at best, but had big boobs. She kept going on about how proud she was of him and how they should celebrate him turning his life around. My ears started to hurt.

Brett sent me to play outside with a huge, dirty sheepdog tied up out back while he celebrated being sober and doing the right thing. That dog was one mean S.O.B. and wanted nothing to do with me. He just ran around in a circle as far as the chain would let him go. He kept barking and snapping at me when I tried to reach for his toys. I read that some dogs don't like kids. I got bit by a dog once before. I don't remember much, except having to tell one of the nuns whose dog it was. They had to go to talk to the owner to check if the dog had all of its shots.

It was getting dark. I was bored out of my mind and was getting eaten up by mosquitoes, so I went back inside to grab my bow and arrows from Brett's room so I could shoot at the dog. Brett wasn't there. I grabbed my plastic bag and ate one of my Snickers bars before my target practice out back.

I ended up getting the dog good, once in the eye. At the time, I felt that the bastard deserved it, but I feel bad about it now. He was dirty, angry, and his small world was only as far as the length of that chain that choked him. He was probably starving. The losers at that house couldn't take care of themselves; there was no way they should have had pets *or* children.

After another hour my last arrow fell in the range of the dog's chain, so I wasn't getting it back. I was really getting bit up by bugs and was bored out of my mind. I was getting sick of listening to the Grateful Dead blast from the house. I don't care how high you are, how can anyone listen to "Casey Jones" that many times in a row?

I tried to get back inside, but the door was locked.

I knocked.

Sunshine answered and looked a lot different. In hindsight, I see that she was drugged out of her mind. I asked if I could come in.

"Just leave us alone, kid," Sunshine said.

"Can I talk to Brett?" I asked.

Sunshine told me he wasn't there, even though I could hear him in the background. At least I thought I heard him in the background; he sounded so different that I couldn't even be sure 100% if it was him.

"I can hear him," I said.

Sunshine slammed the door in my face.

"Kids are such a pain!"

I didn't really know what the hell was going on back then, but it was obvious Brett was ditching me. What a shit loser he was/is.

I was getting hungry, so I chowed down on my other Snickers bar.

It was too dark to read my *Amazing Spider-Man* comic and the dog looked to be sleeping, so I decided to go for some of my arrows. As soon as I reached for one, the dog launched towards me. I was in shock and couldn't move. The dog clamped down on my forearm. He drew blood.

That's the second time I ever got bit by a dog. Luckily, he let go quickly.

I knocked on the back door again, only to have

Sunshine dump a half-empty can of beer with snuffed out cigarettes in it on my head. Brett laughed his ass off, being torn up from smoking crack and drinking.

After a few hours of waiting outside, I decided to hitchhike back to the orphanage. I would never see Brett or Sunshine again.

Some couple that was headed back to the city picked me up. Nice people, but nothing much to mention.

The worst part is, I never got to tell him off. He stole that from me. I hope he dies a slow and painful death, if he isn't dead already.

When I got back to the orphanage, Dinker and Peewee were waiting for me on the front steps. All the other kids had either gone to bed or were playing Nintendo, but my brother and sister were there waiting for me. I needed that.

I tried to be upbeat, but that's difficult to do when you smell like an ashtray and booze. I didn't wanna talk about how my day with Brett went, I just wanted to forget about it. I told them about the Manahawkin Indians and then I promised them I would always keep the pact. We were always going to be family. We gave each other a giant group hug and I gave them the Snickers bar that I stole. They didn't ask anything about Brett.

CHAPTER 13
The Nintendo Gold Card

It was cold. I know for a fact that any people farther north than New Jersey have it rough in the winter. I also know for a fact that the homeless have it worse than we orphans did—no one is saying they don't—but to us orphans no heat in February in New Jersey was the worst.

I was wrapped up in a moth-eaten wool blanket, sitting next to Peewee on the floor with our Nintendo controllers and playing *Super Mario Bros.* I was playing and Peewee was watching. He would move his fingers on the controller like he was playing though. My fingers were stiff from the cold and the blanket kept sliding off of my hands. Another game for us would have meant playing till sunrise, but for now, *The Mushroom Kingdom* from *Super Mario Bros.* on the TV screen was the only thing lighting up the room.

There had been quite a few changes in rank since Christmas. Dennis had new rules for who got to play the Nintendo and when. Ultimately, I think Peewee was the one who got the ball moving on what you would call "reform" and what we orphans would call "doing things the hard way."

Peewee asked, "Why in the blue hell are we playing so late on a school night?"

"You know why," I said.

Peewee gave the kind of groan you're only capable of giving in the early morning; it was just a low-pitched rumble practically coming from his chest.

"I hate the older kids and their stupid cards. Who made them in charge? And who decides who gets a card to play when they want to and forces the rest of us to wait? It's BS, if you ask me."

Peewee shook his head, tsking. I don't know where he picked up tsking, but he sure as hell was doing a lot of it then.

We switched the game to hockey. I called dibs on the Canadian team.

The game started and I scored right off from the face-off. Peewee was clearly getting cranky. I was really good at goaltending in this game

"Come on!" Peewee whined.

After a while Peewee was getting sleepy. He kept doing those blinks that were just a bit too long, so I kept scoring.

"The only reason you win is because I'm always sleepy," Peewee said. "We shouldn't have to stay up so late to play. The only reason we all have a Nintendo is because of you anyway."

As far as those new rules Dennis had made, and one thing I haven't mentioned yet: The orphanage was a very "What have you done for me lately?" type of place. Even though I got the Nintendo, I'd lost proper privilege to play ever since I had hung out with Brett that one day. A lot of people lost respect for me.

Leaving with a parent was like betraying them. You don't betray your own kind. You don't defect.

"I'm going to get another card tomorrow," I told Peewee.

"Really?"

"Yeah, why not?" "That's awesome."

Peewee put the controller down and stood up.

"Where you going?"

"To bed," he said, yawning.

He then reached for the Reset button, but I grabbed him. "What the hell are you doing?"

"I'm resetting it and going to bed."

"What?! Do you want to be known as a resetter?"

"Heck, no."

"There are only five minutes left. Let me just finish."

Peewee shrugged, acting like it was no big deal, but I knew for a fact he didn't want this game to go on his record. He wanted to reset the game so badly. He ended up heading to bed anyway and I played the last five minutes of the game, trying to score as many goals as I could.

The sun was starting to come up. I could've gone to bed and got one or two hours of sleep, but now the Triforce was calling and it sure as hell wasn't going to collect itself. I popped in *The Legend of Zelda*.

I had a love-hate relationship with Dennis. The rules sucked, but it was better to have early morning Nintendo than no Nintendo at all. Plus, thanks to Dennis no one dared delete a saved game. And no one except me played *The Legend of Zelda*, so those saved files were all I had.

The next day after school I heard people moving the beds around in the boys' room. I thought something was fishy from the get-go, but when they started chanting my name, I knew I was in trouble.

When I went into the room, there was a gladiator pit made with metal bunk beds, and orphans were sitting on both the bottom and top bunks cheering me on. It felt like the Coliseum or Madison Square Garden, but in a very, very bad way. I was screwed.

Dennis, the toughest kid in the orphanagewas waiting for me. He pointed at me like he was Hulk Hogan ready to kick my ass.

"You want a card? Come get it."

Damn you, Peewee-rican! You and your damn big

mouth!

To get a permission card to play the Nintendo you had to last ten minutes in a wrestling match against one of the older kids. Someone would keep track of the time on an old oven timer.

The match started before I even knew it. Dennis beat me down like I owed him money. The crowd loved every second of it. Somehow, during my butt whoopin', Dennis got me in his special move, The Dennis Boston Crab. I was lying on my stomach. Dennis sat on my back while trying to double my legs over me. The worst part was the wiener punching. That was the cherry on top of Dennis's Boston Crab. It was pure agony.

It was then that I looked up to see how much time was left. I only had one more minute. Then I saw who was holding the clock. Peewee. He looked at me with this dead expression on his face and turned the timer back six minutes.

Under any other circumstances, I would've thrown a beating to him after seeing him do something like that. But because of the no-hands bike incident last year, I let it go.

I tried to fake extra pain in hopes that Dennis might ease up on me, but it was no good. He was giving me his best, or his worst, depending on how you look at it.

That fight lasted forever. It wouldn't surprise me one bit if Peewee had turned the timer back another two or three times somewhere during that ass beating I got. The big surprise for me was that the bell ended up ringing at all, but it finally did.

I had done my time in the ring. I would get my card. I was so happy, I forgot all about Peewee. Maybe I would earn my respect back after all.

Well, my glory didn't last long, because a few weeks later the older kids made a new system where there was a gold card, and my card was only good for a certain time, and someone with a gold card could bump you off to play at any time. What a corrupt operation they had going.

One day me and Dinker were watching Peewee fight Mike Tyson on *Punch-Out!!* Peewee was on fire. His game was the best I had ever seen. At that point in my life I had never seen anyone ever beat Mike Tyson. Bucky said that some kid named Jimmy Black, who lived a couple of towns over, beat Tyson, but I'd have had to see it to believe it.

"I'd have to see it to believe it." That saying always was one to piss off Sister Satan.

Peewee took Tyson into the third and last round. In between rounds Doc mumbled some advice as Peewee held down the Select button with all his might. Me and Dinker were cheering our hearts out. I'd never gotten past the first few punches before Tyson knocked me out. Peewee hit Start and his energy bar went up. If we hadn't seen it right then, we'd have never believed it.

Peewee was in a war with Kid Dynamite and I felt, in my heart, his time was now.

That's when Dennis and his crew came in and made their claim. "Gold cards only!"

"That's not fair!" Dinker screamed. "He's going to beat Tyson!"

When Dinker said the Tyson part, everyone within earshot came to huddle around the TV. Peewee was in the zone. People started crowding, but still made sure to give Peewee enough breathing room. I think he was getting nervous.

"No one can beat Tyson. Everyone knows the game is rigged." Dennis said.

"Jimmy Black did!" Bucky shouted from beside Peewee.

"That's baloney!" Dennis said back.

Dennis ignored the pleas of everyone who wanted to finally witness Mike Tyson getting KO'd. He purposely bumped into Peewee and reached to turn off the game. Tyson slugged Little Mac, putting him down. The referee, Mario, came out and started the count. Peewee was smashing those buttons as hard as he could to get Mac back up. The crowd surrounding the television was huge now with game-lovers and rubberneckers. We were practically crying to Dennis to let Peewee finish the game.

"Please, just let him finish!" I said. "If the game is rigged like you say, Peewee will be knocked out in less than ten seconds anyway."

Referee Mario was on the screen, still counting 6....7....8....

Peewee smashed those buttons like his life depended on it.

9! And Mac was up! Little Mac was up! Everyone went bonkers.

Dennis hated to have his authority challenged. Hell, isn't that the story of everyone who has authority in the history of the world ever? That they have to have it challenged?

"Why should I?" Dennis said, sneering.

"I'll make a bet with ya," I said. No one from New Jersey can resist a bet.

"Go on…"

"If Peewee wins, you have to give us a gold card and make no more higher cards than gold."

"And if he loses?"

"I don't know. What do you want? My soul!?"

"That's not worth much. How 'bout you pick all the weed in the back so Sister Satan will get off my back!"

"Done and done," I said.

We shook on it. The excitement in the room could probably only be matched by a World Cup game in Brazil, or like when the New Jersey Devils were in the Stanley Cup Finals. Peewee was so nervous, he was sweating. He had less than one minute to shock our world, and his fingers were slipping like banana peels on that controller.

Tyson kept missing with his punches and Peewee was landing a ton of punches with Mac, but still couldn't lay any serious damage on Iron Mike. Peewee went for a headshot, but his timing was off and Tyson caught him with a right hook. Peewee's life bar was down to a sliver now. Seriously, there had to be only two pixels of life for Peewee on that TV.

There were only ten seconds left.

Dinker offered some encouragement.

"Play it safe. If you fall, you won't be able to get back up."

It was enough to motivate Peewee, though, because he was dodging everything Mike was throwing at him now.

The bell rang, bringing the third and final round to an end. We all went crazy except for Dennis, who had to make it known to everyone that the game was rigged and Tyson always wins.

It went to a decision. Mike Tyson in the upper-right corner and a tiny and beaten Little Mac on the bottom of the screen. The score said 4900, but no one knew what the hell that meant. Mario walked out from the right. It's moments like these where you always feel time stopping. The room was frozen. No one had ever made it this far. What the hell was gonna happen? We all sat there with our mouths open like we were letting the flies in.

Mario gave the decision and pointed to Mike Tyson. Peewee fell to his knees, covering up for a second or two, and then ran out of the room. Dinker followed him, but made sure to bump into Dennis on the way out. Dennis normally wouldn't let anyone get away with something like that—and I mean anyone—but he liked Dinker for her spunky attitude.

"Jimmy Black could beat 'im," Bucky said again.

Well, me and Peewee ended up weeding the entire backyard and it sucked! If you had to look at it from a glass half-full perspective, I can say that at least it was starting to warm up outside. Also, Dinker helped her brothers out of the goodness of her heart. Peewee was crushed and had been keeping mostly to himself ever since the *Punch-Out!!* incident.

Dinker kept talking about how Peewee could have won if it wasn't for Dennis and his stupid gold cards. After a few hours, and experiencing my first backache, some of the nuns came out and thanked us for doing a good job. I just thanked God that Sister Satan wasn't there that time or she would have had us on something else sooner than you could say, "Cowabunga!"

We were tired and dirty. Inside, we walked by Dennis as he was glowing with joy playing *Pro Wrestling*, a game he stole. He was playing as a pink-masked wrestler named Starman and was beating down a green monster called The Amazon. Peewee and Dinker just kept walking.

I walked up to Dennis from an angle where he could see me. I tried to talk low so Peewee and Dinker wouldn't hear.

"What do I have to do to get a gold card?"

"What?" Dennis asked, still absorbed in his game.

"What do I have to do to get a gold card? Fight someone again?"

"Psh, right. I'm tired of whooping your butt," he said and laughed. "Gold cards are reserved for the strong and brave."

"Want me to kiss Sister Satan?"

I said it as a joke and was praying he wouldn't take me up on it. The joke worked. Dennis and his older orphan friends chuckled.

Dennis put his arm around me. "You hate Santa, right?" "You know I do."

"Burn down the Santa billboard you always see when you enter AC."

I gave it a good thought or two, and decided to agree to it only under two conditions: one, the gold card would be the highest level from then on, and two, me, Peewee, and Dinker would all get gold cards.

Surprisingly, Dennis agreed and I went on my way, and he went back to throwing a beatdown on The Amazon.

"Do you think that was a good idea?" one of his cronies asked.

"They won't burn down shit," I heard Dennis mumble.

Dennis should have taken himself more seriously.


The next morning, I told Peewee and Dinker what we had to do to get gold cards. Peewee was on board and would do anything for just one more shot at Tyson in front of all the other  kids. I turned to Dinker, thinking she was going to be against it. Little did I know, Dinker  was a freakin' pyro. She had a huge smile on her face.

"I got everything we'll need. This is going to be great," she said.

"You already have everything?" I asked.
"I love burning. It makes me feel good inside." Kids say the darndest things.

"Really?" I was seriously concerned. I couldn't believe I knew nothing of this side of Dinker until now. I knew she was kind of sadistic, but wow . . .

Dinker giggled. "Remember that shed fire?"

"That was you?"

"That was me!"

"But I was blamed for that and got a beating from Sister Satan!"

Dinker kept laughing. "That was me!"

I can't believe none of that even fazed Peewee.

At that point, we'd snuck out so many times, we didn't even put much thought into it anymore. Later that night we borrowed some black clothing and made the long trek out to the billboard that Dennis was talking about. It was a simple mission: climb up, spread gasoline, and set the damn thing on fire.

Peewee was the most nervous out of the three of us. He just wanted to get it over with and get the hell out of there, which was the opposite of what Dinker was trying to do. She wanted to savor every moment.

Well, we tried lighting it, but with no success. It was cold and windy as hell and we were really high up. It never looks as high until you actually climb it. Also, it was so hard to hear anyone talk because of the cars zipping down below us, plus the wind. We took a break to admire the scenery. The view of the city was beautiful at night. Before I even got to appreciate the view, Peewee started to climb down. He was giving up. I didn't know what to do either. That billboard was not lighting, even with the gasoline.

"Take officer!" Dinker shouted, and I gave her a funny look because I didn't know if I heard her right or not. Her words were being thrown everywhere but in my direction. "TAKE OFF A SOCK!" she shouted again.

Okay, I heard her that time, but now my foot was gonna be cold, I thought. I pulled off my sock and Dinker dunked the sock in the gasoline—oddly enough, it was the sock I got from jolly old Saint Nick. Dinker lit it up. It caught fire instantly, and then the billboard caught too. Before the sock burned completely, it was blown away by the strong wind. The billboard woofed like a dog and the flames started sweeping at us. The heat was intense and that thing was probably visible for miles, so we started rushing to climb down. Hopefully, three kids running home wearing all black wouldn't raise any red flags.

Small pieces of lit billboard hit me on the way down, but nothing big enough to burn me. The wind kicked in every now and then, pushing the flames in one direction or another.

We ran home, looking back every now and then to admire our handiwork. The fire was nearly out now.

In the end, only the bottom of the billboard really

caught, and the damage was fixed in less than a week, but that wasn't the problem: it was that damn sock. The wind ended up carrying that freaking thing all the way to some abandoned warehouse's roof. When me, Peewee, and Dinker were nearly home, a huge explosion went off.

I think Peewee always felt guilty about it because he never could follow up on any news about the incident. But that building was actually being used to make illegal drugs—it was AC's biggest meth lab operation at the time. The fire torched the roof, and once it made it inside, the place blew sky high. It made all the headlines the next day. We didn't care about the lab burning though; the important thing was the newspaper pictures of the billboard!

But, to think, all that trouble over a damn sock!
Dennis had to honor his word, so me, Peewee, and Dinker all got gold cards.

We started holding regular tournaments and even made newsletters to sell to the other kids. We sold tickets to the Tyson vs. Peewee rematch, where Peewee finally beat the big guy, and we earned enough cash to eat at Pizza Hut without cheating the BOOK IT! program.

Anyone else remember BOOK IT!?

Someone mentioned the cops coming by the orphanage and asking questions about the fire, but I think it was just to try and shake us up. Peewee *was* shaken for a few days, but not about the cops. He was worried that a cat might have died in that fire. Dinker was being Dinker, with maybe a little more joy. She now had a gold card and got to burn a billboard and meth warehouse, probably saving half of the youth in AC from a life of addiction in the process.

# CHAPTER 14
## Lucky vs. Santa


Something from the corner of my eye caught my attention. It was a paper flyer that was drawn by one of the other orphans. It included a message written by the nuns. The picture was done with crayons. Definitely some new kid. You could tell by how cute and innocent it was. It was a drawing of an overweight Santa. I mean, Santa is naturally overweight, but this one was a giant ball of red. Holding Santa's hand was an elf dressed exactly like Santa. I guess it was supposed to be cute, because the kid didn't know yet that elves dressed in green or something. It was no secret that before long, whoever that kid was—and it never mattered *who* you were, it didn't matter how sweet you were—would eventually get on S.S.'s bad side and get a beating.

I got in real close to read the message because it was written in cursive. I hated cursive, though I take pride in my nice signature. I would always pray that one day people would come to their senses and finally drop using cursive. (Unfortunately, by the time they actually decided to do away with cursive I was already out of school.)

The message talked about Santa and one of the cardinals. I couldn't make out which cardinal it was, but apparently a cardinal was coming to visit us at the orphanage. And even though I was surrounded by Catholics 24/7, I had no idea about most of their traditions (other than a nun hat is called a coif and that string of beads they always carry is called a rosary). Due to them not being specific enough, I was expecting to see St. Louis Cardinal Ozzie Smith or something. Something like that wouldn't have been out of the question, after all. On TV they always have celebrities visit orphanages to try and show the world they care about kids that are only gonna grow up to be criminals, or sacrificial soldiers for the state—guilty as charged!

The flyer had the date and time. We only had two days to prepare, but was I ready? It was now or never.

I ripped the flyer down and ran to get Peewee and Dinker. I told them to get everyone in for an emergency meeting in front of the TV. Peewee and Dinker did it the tedious way, flagging kids down one by one. I went straight to Dennis and begged him to round everyone up.

"What are you up to, Lucky? What's this about?" he asked.

"Revenge," I said.

Dennis wasn't in the doing favors business. No one ever was in the doing favors business in the dog-eat-dog world that we lived in. But people from New Jersey hardly ever turned down the opportunity for revenge. Opportunities for revenge are as good as legal tender.

Fact: New Jersey's economy runs on revenge currency. Dennis only needed to snap his fingers, which he did.

At the sound of the snap his cronies rounded everyone up by force in front of the Nintendo for my meeting. I was getting dirty looks, but I didn't care. Once everyone was gathered, the big question came up: What the hell was all this about?

Dennis raised his hand.

"This is about Lucky's plan for revenge!"

They started smiling at the sound of the word alone, *revenge*. They didn't even know the whos or the whats yet. I stood there and held up that small, crappy handmade flyer drawn by one of the orphans. I got some confused looks, but didn't say anything just then. It was a simple ploy. I was building drama and feeling the crowd. It's pretty basic psychological stuff, really.

Dennis scratched his head, looked at the flyer, and then looked out at a group of kids as confused as he was.

"What? You want to beat up the kid who drew this?"

Jeez, I'll bet whoever drew that was out there in the crowd sweating bullets! Ha-ha!

"No, no, no," I said.

"How does that have anything to do with revenge?!" I give Dennis a lot of credit, but sometimes he could be as dumb as a box of rocks.

"We're going to kill Santa Claus!"

Someone started cheering before realizing no one else was cheering with him. He shut up real quick and the room went quiet again.

"Why? He gives us gifts!" someone shouted.

Dennis raised his hand again.

"Lucky, why are we going to kill Santa?"

"For revenge." I tried to stress the word *revenge* as much as I could, hoping that the word alone would be a sort of call to arms.

"Revenge?"

I cleared my throat. It was time for me to be the leader that all these lost dopes needed. They were the lost souls and I was gonna give them purpose by changing the world and making Santa pay for his wrongdoings. In my head, I thought that if Santa fell, it would strike fear in the eyes of the nuns and all others who had done us wrong.

"Santa only delivers the good toys to the rich," I said. A few nodded in the crowd.

"Is that fair?" I asked, looking at the kids who were nodding.

"No!" they hollered out together.

"Santa is worse than those bastards who gave up on us and left us here to die."

Dennis was intrigued, but still doubtful. "How is he worse than our parents?"

There was a hush over the crowd, as Dennis had used one of the P-words.

I started swinging a right hook in the air all high and mighty.

"I'll tell you how! He gave up on us, but still wants us to jump through hoops! We have to be good, but get crap compared to the rich, spoiled ones that have a mom and dad. THAT IS NOT RIGHT!"

Everyone looked like they were on board, but I wanted to bring the point home, or maybe I was just starving for the attention.

"Santa wants us to jump through hoops by being fools who are good all year long. I don't know about you, but I am done jumping! The fat man dies in two days!"

I had their full attention now. Orphans gathered in close to listen. It was the biggest huddle I was ever a part of. Santa in two days? We'd be an army by then!

*** 

And when the day finally came, we were ready. There was only one thing we weren't prepared for, and that was how many people were gonna be at the orphanage, not even for Santa, but the cardinal! There were tons of people dressed in their Sunday best on a Wednesday. There was a ton of media with cameras of all sizes, fuzzy mics, and bright lights. All this and Santa wasn't even the star of the show.

Dinker looked down in the dumps that day. I talked to her, wanting to make sure she was still on board with the assassination. She sighed, and told me she had plans for today other than just killing Santa.

"But you *will* help us kill Santa, right?" I asked.

"Sure," she said, but with not much heart.

I must have given her a look or something because she looked at me before adding one more thing. "You can always count on me, Lucky."

Dinker stayed outside the room as a lookout. The rest of us were waiting in the boys' sleep area. We took out all the light bulbs, and taped black construction paper that someone had stolen from the school's supply closet to the windows to make the room pitch black. It almost looked kinda like Biggie's basement, which was appropriate, because Santa was gonna get his ass beat.

The beds were adjusted so Santa would have nowhere to run when we started the beating.

The orphanage didn't trust us with metal or wooden bats, but we all had brooms, garden tools, and bright yellow wiffle ball bats.

Everyone had their war faces on except Peewee, who was damn near on the brink of tears.

"Lucky, please stop this. You can stop this. We can't do this!" he was saying.

He started to cry, but made sure not to make enough sound for anyone to notice.

"Please, Santa is a good guy. He doesn't deserve this."

I put my hand on Peewee's shoulder. For a second he must have been thinking it was to console him. I whispered, "This is *gonna* happen, no matter what."

Peewee took some deep breaths to calm himself down and then nodded his head. Dinker ran into the room with a huge smile on her face.

"He's coming! The fat bastard is coming and he's alone." Dinker skidded to a stop and turned to close the door.

I thought to myself how easy it was going to be, getting

Santa. It was almost unfair. But what was fair anymore? Santa ripped us off, he deserved whatever was coming to him.

Loud bootsteps were getting closer and closer. The door opened. "Ho-ho-ho!" Santa said.

The room was pitch black. Not even the light coming from the hall was enough to help him see anything. His eyes weren't adjusted to the dark like ours. We all heard him say, "What the hell?" as his hand was rubbing the wall, trying to find the light switch or something. I never smiled so hard in my life.

"Is anyone in here? . . ."

I screamed, "Now!"

Too bad no one could flip on the lights. I would've loved to see the look on Santa's face at that moment when we pounced and beat him down. It was like those nature films you see with the lions at night surrounding an elephant. The elephant always senses the lions are there, but it doesn't know where they are exactly, and the film is all green because it's in night vision and all the lions' eyes are shining. Then a lion sinks its teeth in the elephant's rear. Then the elephant tries to hobble away, but the rest of the group just takes it down.

And what did Santa sound like when we took him down? A crying elephant.

I couldn't see the blood, but I could feel it on my face. A few of the kids in the back accidentally hit kids in front of them. Like I said, it was dark as all hell, but besides that, we were a perfect machine of beating and devouring.

Santa was screaming for help, but no one could hear him because they were all downstairs with that cardinal. Everything was going wonderfully.

Those sticks hitting him with all us chanting, "Die, Santa, die!" It sounded like some kinda death choir.

"I'm not Santa!" he cried.

A clever trick, of course. We continued to wail on Santa, who was now curling up into a ball. I never saw an adult do this until then, what they call the fetal position.

"I swear I'm not Santa!" he yelled.

"Yeah, right!" Some kids in the back ran to the windows and ripped down the paper and let the sunshine in.

Covered in blood, in a Santa suit, and wearing a fake beard was . . . Father O'Touches-a-lot. I didn't care about O.T., my priority was the mission. Where the hell was Santa?

I grabbed O.T. by the collar.

"Where the hell is the real Santa and why are you helping him?!"

O.T. pulled the crooked fake beard from his face and snapped it under his chin.

"There is no goddamn Santa!"

"Huh?"

"Santa is not real, you sons of bitches! You no-good bastards!"

I couldn't tell if he was crying or yelling. It was probably a little bit of both. I couldn't believe I just heard Father O'Touches-a-lot use the words *goddamn, bitches,* and *bastards*. I guess you can beat the religion out of anyone.

Everyone was slack-jawed at the sight of O.T.

There was a hush over us, a shock that we had been lied to. All of us lied to by so many. Not to mention, Father O'Touches-a-lot cursing up a storm. I guess that helped reality sink in too.

O.T. slowly got up on one knee and Dinker smashed him over the head with a metal pipe she would later tell me she found under the sink. He fell hard to the ground. Blood started flowing out from the back of his head. We all thought he was dead. This would be our second reality check.

It wasn't Santa and for all we knew at the time, there might not be a Santa at all. Then who in the hell was screwing us all along?

We all looked to Dinker, horrified. She was still holding the pipe and we didn't know if she was finished or not.

Dinker didn't utter a word. She took a few seconds to stare at the bloody O.T., shrugged, and then just walked off with what I swear was a bounce in her step. I guess she thought that the incident would all be swept under the rug in an hour or two.

I was trying to think of something to do, but everyone was too shaken up. We all knew what we were getting into before it happened, but need I remind you, we were only kids. Kids rarely ever have a plan B. We didn't know what to do next.

S.S. ran in, saw bloody O.T., and went into hysterical mode. We still had all of our weapons in our hands.

Caught red-handed, as they say.

I was closest to Father O.T., which is why, I guess, S.S. singled me out.

"This is all your fault, Devil Child!"

## CHAPTER 15
### Lucky vs. Sister Satan

Sister Satan pulled me down the hall by my ear and every time I squirmed to try to get free, she beat me with an open palm like she was a giant bear. It hurt like hell. I knew I was screwed. Peewee, Dennis, Bucky, and some of the others followed close by with a scared look in their eyes. It was the first time I ever saw Dennis look scared.

Sister Satan took me via the back stairs so none of the news stations or the cardinal would see us. Other nuns were pleading with S.S. to let me go.

"Just keep these other brats back!" she ordered them. "I swear to God, I'm going to kill this boy."

She shoved me into a small room where they made the morning and evening announcements, and out came that ruler. The door never closed though. That sadistic bitch wanted the other orphans to watch. She had me in the corner. She whipped the ruler at me and broke it on my face, which made me laugh and still does. That laughing didn't do me any good because then she started beating me down with anything she could grab.

One of the nuns nervously mentioned, "What about the cardinal?! You can't do this with the cardinal here!"

Sister Satan let me be for nine seconds as she slapped the nun with the big mouth and said, "Catholic men are worthless thieves! We do all the dirty work of the Lord!"

By this time, Peewee and the others had pushed their way into the room where S.S. was walloping me. The nuns were now pushing back hard to try and herd Peewee and a few of the others out. Through the chaos and confusion is where Peewee's single stroke of genius happened: as everyone was getting pushed back he switched on the sound system in the room. Now, according to Bucky, he swears that one of the nuns actually saw Peewee flip the switch and yet did nothing. Bucky says that she paused and looked at the button for a second or two, and could have easily turned it off, or at least could have said something. But no. Instead she gave Peewee a quick nod before shoving him out of the room.

The whole building was airing my beatdown on the sound system. If I knew about it ahead of time, I would have sold tickets myself! All the guests, the media, and the cardinal to witness, with their ears, the true "work of the Lord."

Sister Satan's words exactly, "I'm going to kill you for the Lord!" thundered throughout the building.

At the time, I knew as much as S.S. did about the PA system being on. I wasn't acting even though everyone credits me for having "put on a good show." But I guess that can have two meanings. I kept repeating my mantra that Peewee taught me at the top of my lungs. "I am better than you!"

She would slap me down, but I just popped right back up like a Marine at attention, screaming, "I am better than you!"

She started hitting me hard then. I didn't have the strength to stand up anymore and fell to the floor. There was blood dripping down from my nose and mouth. I perked my head up again and screamed, "I am better than you!"

And all this time, what the hell was being done about O.T.? I have no clue, but we already know S.S. didn't really care about him anyway.

Well anyway, the guests, media, and cardinal were panicking, looking for the room.

People were either cheering me on, or cheering the situation on, because I don't know why you'd cheer for the guy who was getting his ass helplessly beat. S.S. wouldn't break my spirit yet, but I was still getting one hell of an ass whoopin'.

She punched me in the gut and I fell over.

"You think you are better than me? You think you are better than the Lord?"

S.S. was breathing heavy and sweating like crazy. I thought to myself, she is beating me and she is more tired than me? I told myself I could take more, but I was fooling myself. I was damn near spent. I didn't know her old bones had so much energy in them.

I took a deep, bloody breath and showed her just how insolent I could be.

"I don't know if there is a Lord. Hell, only a few minutes ago I thought there really was a Santa."

S.S. lightly slapped me. She was just about as gassed out as I was. If I had devoted more energy to actually kicking her ass though, I could've won that day easily. I have no idea why I didn't fight back. Maybe I had something to prove.

"But I know I am better than you," I said.

She lost it and with what energy she had left had a hissy fit of slaps and it felt so good because she couldn't hurt me anymore.

The cardinal busted in like a cheesy superhero with a bad costume. Media, guests, nuns, orphans, and what seemed like everyone in town, including Korean Jen and her family, followed behind. I couldn't see much except the few people in the very front, but everyone told me later that they were there. Somebody pulled Sister Satan off of me and I have no idea who.

The cardinal stood next to me. Bright lights blinded me. All the eyes and cameras were on us. I felt so weak and embarrassed. Some of the orphans clapped. All of the adults were just horrified by what they were seeing. The cardinal kneeled down and asked me my name.

"Lucky," I said in what may have well been a whisper.

The cardinal began preaching about forgiveness and how he was going to fix the broken system.

Dinker ruined the good moment when she squeezed through, got in front of the camera, and screamed, "Shut up, old man!"

There was silence. Only Dinker could steal the show from a cardinal. She later would tell me that what I did gave her strength to do what she was about to do.
She had the world listening to her and that was all she needed to be saved.

"You and all of yous," she said, pointing at the nuns and media. "Are you gonna do nothing? I told you all about Father O'Touches-a-lot and what he does to me, and all of you did *nothing*. Nothing, I say. You all knew this woman beat us and you all knew about Father O'Touches-a-lot. Every single one of you! I told you all and you all did *nothing*!"

Dinker looked like she had the DT shakes.

Now the cardinal was already kneeling, but it looked almost like he took another knee before scooping up Dinker to give her a big hug. He thanked her for being brave, then asked, "What happened here? What did he do to you?"

Dinker was shy, but still brave. She whispered in the cardinal's ear.

Hey, what about me, I thought. But I didn't know about O.T. abusing Dinker at that time.

When Dinker was done whispering, the cardinal smiled at her. Dinker today claims that the cardinal was the kindest man she had ever met. He raised his hand and promised he would fix everything and guaranteed us orphans safety. Peewee finally snuck through the crowd and we all hugged each other.

***

That night, and the next day, the news was broadcast throughout the city. Some protesters showed up at the orphanage, but after a day or two it was forgotten about, just like the warehouse fire earlier in the year.

Father O'Touches-a-lot didn't die. He went to the hospital and ended up transferring to another church. None of us orphans ever saw O.T. again. Life is funny sometimes. O.T.'s punishment for pretending to be Santa Claus was worse than for what he did to Dinker behind closed doors.

The night after the beating, Sister Satan locked herself in the room and drank and doped herself to death. Everyone said it was a suicide, and since S.S. killed herself, she won't get into heaven. God can be a real dick sometimes.

No one mentioned Father O'Touches-a-lot ever again and Sister Satan taking her own life was practically celebrated by all, orphans and nuns.

Dennis and others congratulated me as if I had slayed a giant dragon or killed Darth Vader. Everyone once again treated me like I was a hero, but inside I felt kinda bad about Sister Satan. Sometimes answered prayers become more of a problem than what things were like to begin with.

***

I went to Sister Satan's funeral. It was the most depressing thing I have ever been to. There was no one there but me and her dead body. They didn't fix her up. She was still in the same clothes she died in, no make up, and no flowers, just her in the cheapest casket someone could find. I worried for a few minutes that they were just going to chuck her in some landfill.

I hated this woman with all my heart, but she deserved better than that. It felt awkward with no priest, nuns, friends, or family. Dinker and Peewee wouldn't even join me, though

146

you can't blame them. I even tried to ask a nun to be with me and maybe say a prayer. "She was a horrible person," was the only answer I got.

I was alone in that huge empty room, looking down on a very ugly Sister Satan. I mean, she was always ugly, but after a few days of being dead, she looked like a monster from those late-night horror movies Peewee loved so much.

I felt the need to say something to her, so I did.

"I'm sure others will come soon. I think there was a mix up on the. . ."

I stopped myself and asked myself, why the hell am I lying to a dead person?

"S.S., we hated each other. If I'm the reason you did this, I'm really really sorry."

I went to touch her hand, but thought twice about it. I settled on leaning on the coffin instead.

"I never really wanted this. Okay, well, maybe I did a little."

My God, she looked hideous.

"Okay, maybe a lot, but you know how you were."

I thought it was weird that I wasn't crying. Little did I know, I would never cry at funerals. Kinda makes me wonder if something is broken inside me.

"You know I never saw you happy. I hope your God lets you into heaven and you can finally be happy."

I started to pray or at least do something I thought was praying.

"Dear God. . ."

I have no freaking idea why I started it that way. Like it was a letter.

"This is Lucky—like you didn't know already? If it's not too late, please forgive Sister Satan so you can like, let her into Heaven or something. Amen."

I tried to imagine that God was actually listening to me, but I didn't really believe stuff like that worked then. It sure as hell doesn't work now either. What I did was more for my own piece of mind than anything. I shrugged my shoulders. I was at a loss for words. I dug into my pockets for something to give to her.

"I just want you to know that I don't hate you like I thought I did. I'm sorry, and I hope you found happiness."

I pulled out a Snickers bar and gave it to her.

"I paid for that one," I said.

For the second time that day, I lied to a dead person. As I walked out slowly I turned to give her one more look. I had said my peace.

*** 

The next night me, Peewee, and Dinker were huddled around the Nintendo to watch Peewee battle Tyson again. He was getting really good at that game. Little Mac knocked out Iron Mike and we were the happiest we had been in days. Peewee was beating Tyson, S.S. and O.T. were gone, and we had gold cards and were the heroes of the orphanage.

Peewee asked, "What now?"

"I don't know. You wanna play *Super Mario Bros.*?" Dinker asked.

"*Ice Hockey*!" I said. "Dibs on Killers!"
"You always play the Killers!" Peewee moaned.

"That's because they have more heart!"

"Lucky?" Dinker asked. "Whatever happens if your dad decides to come back?"

It was the first time any of us had mentioned Brett since that day he showed up.

I looked to Dinker and Peewee and put down the controller. I remember wanting to say that I hoped Brett was taking a long drive off a short pier somewhere, but instead I said, "Nothing. I've got the only family I'll ever need right here."

I leaned in, arms open, and gave my brother and sister the biggest hug I ever gave anyone.

# About the Authors

Ray Fisher is from Northeastern/Central Pennsylvania. He studied music in California and currently resides in Tokyo, Japan.

Dave Koco, originally from the United States, served in the Marine Corps Infantry for four years. He now lives in Tokyo, Japan. He is the father of three children.

Ray and Dave are also co-authors of the action adventure/thriller novel, *Operation Freakshow*.

www.ingramcontent.com/pod-product-compliance
Lightning Source LLC
Chambersburg PA
CBHW031254060726

47590CB00003B/903